The Upstair

Chapter One

Once the mad rush of the summer season was over
Monday morning was usually fairly quiet in the tearoom. I
put this down to it being what I called a 'changeover' day. In
low season people, who were able to, tended to take
advantage of short break deals offered by the tourist industry;
this meant that on Mondays the 'weekenders' were on their
way home and the 'mid-weekers' usually only arrived after
lunch and were settling in.

Olive could normally manage what custom we did have
on her own while I took the opportunity to do some baking
and catch up with the jobs that tend to get pushed to one side
when we're busy. I was putting a batch of scones into the
oven when I saw the delivery van pull up by the back gate.
Thank goodness. I'd put the order into the wholesalers a few
days ago not realising until then how low we'd become on
basic essentials such as tea, coffee and sugar. I went out to
open the gate to allow the delivery man to wheel the boxes
into the yard on his trolley. "By the back door, Harriet?" he
asked.

"Yes please, Phil." I said, "have you time for a cuppa?"

He pulled his face and shook his head. "Unfortunately
not. I'm rushed off my feet today; we've got two drivers off
sick but thanks for the offer."

I locked the gate behind him when he left and went to find
Olive. She was serving a customer but we weren't busy.

"Our delivery has just arrived" I said, "I'll take the boxes upstairs."

"Do you need a hand?" she asked.

"No thanks I can manage."

I left a couple of the heavier boxes in the downstairs store room to be unpacked later but took the rest upstairs. When the last one was neatly piled on top of the others in a corner of the main room I took a few minutes to catch my breath.

The upstairs rooms were accessed by a staircase between the tearoom and the kitchen and comprised two decent sized rooms, one of which had been partitioned off to allow a bathroom to be installed. The previous owners of The Toasted Bun had lived over the shop, as had I when I first took over the business but it had always been temporary as I needed somewhere bigger for when the family visited.

I had left a large family home so I had to put most of my furniture into storage and even when I moved into my cottage there was still too much but rather than pay to keep the rest of it in storage I brought it to the flat. My daughter, Naiomi, had suggested that I rent out the flat as a holiday let but because the only access was through the tearooms I dismissed the idea as impractical. I was suddenly jolted out of my reverie by a voice from downstairs.

"Harriet, I think your scones are burning!" shouted Olive.

Oh heck I'd forgotten all about them.

A couple of days later I was surprised to see Kathleen Thomas come into the tearoom and take a seat at one of the tables; she was a regular customer but not usually on a Wednesday morning. I went over to take her order.

"Good morning, Kathleen, we don't normally see you on a Wednesday morning; I thought you went to the knitting circle in the village hall."

Her face took on a sad expression. "I used to but we've had to disband the group."

"That's a shame" I said, "I expect you'll really miss it."

"You're telling me," she said, rolling her eyes. "Since Fred's mum came to live with us it's been the highlight of my week. Not that we don't get on, I love her to bits but she can be quite demanding at times and the knitting circle was an escape."

I sat down opposite her. "Why has it been disbanded?"

Kathleen sighed. "They've put the rent up for the room and we can't afford it. There's only six of us at the moment and it's simply too much."

"Oh I see."

While she'd been speaking an idea had been running around in my brain. "I might be able to help." I said.

"Really? How?"

"Well, the flat upstairs is lying empty now and you could meet in there. There is some furniture already up there but I'm sure we could get some more if needed."

Her mood started to lift. "That sounds promising."

"I'll take your order and give it to Olive" I said "and while she's getting it ready I'll take you upstairs and you can have a look."

"Fantastic" she said.

I took her into what had once been the living room. "As you can see there is a sofa and a couple of armchairs, a coffee table and a couple of hard backed dining chairs. I'm sure we could get some more comfy chairs if we asked around."

The smile on Kathleen's face told me she was interested.

"I'd move the boxes to the other room of course but there is a bathroom and toilet so you wouldn't need to come down and use the one in the cafe."

"This would be perfect," she said. "How much would you be asking for a morning's rent?"

"Nothing" I said.

Her eyebrows shot into her hairline. "Nothing? Are you sure? You're doing yourself out of some regular added income."

"But I'm thinking you'll be buying your refreshments from downstairs so that would increase my takings which would be a good help in the quiet season."

"Harriet Jones, I could kiss you," she said. "In fact I will!"

She turned and grabbed me into a tight hug which nearly took my breath away and slapped a smacking kiss on my left cheek. When she released me I burst out laughing. "I take it you'll be here next Wednesday morning then."

"Abso-flipping-lutely" she said; "wait until I tell the others."

"I'll give the curtains a wash" I said, "to brighten the room up a bit."

"And I'll get Fred to come in and give the walls a lick of paint," said Kathleen. "He'll have it done in a jiffy seeing as how he does it for a living and he'll probably have some paint he can use so it won't cost anything."

Chapter Two

Kathleen was as good as her word and early the next day Fred turned up with all his gear, several tins of emulsion and his mate, Dave, to help him. It only took them a couple of hours and they refused any payment so I told them to sit down for a Full English on the house. Olive served the two men their breakfasts and we left them in peace to eat but when they'd finished Fred's mate Dave came to the counter to speak to me. "Thanks for the breakfast but I did have an ulterior motive for helping Fred" he said.

"Oh yes" I said, "what's that?"

"I belong to a book club and we're also having to leave the village hall because of the rent so I was wondering if we could use the room on Tuesday afternoons."

"Yes of course" I said "but will you have enough seats?"

"Oh Kathleen's already on to that" said Fred coming up behind his friend. "She's picked up a couple of chairs from one of the charity shops and a couple of her friends have got spares they're willing to donate."

"That's wonderful" I said. "I'll see you next Tuesday then Dave."

"You certainly will," he said.

The word was getting around about my upstairs room and I was approached by a creative writing group and a group of ladies who wanted to start a cardmaking group.

"I think we'd better get a diary," I said to Olive, "so we can keep a check on who is booked in and when so we don't double up."

Olive was never one to shy away from voicing her opinion on anything but she had been unusually quiet about my opening up the upstairs room and I was beginning to wonder if this was a sign that she didn't approve but I couldn't have been more wrong because she said "These groups using upstairs will be good for business, especially in the low season."

"I thought of that myself," I said. "They won't bring in a fortune but it'll keep us ticking over in the Winter and it's good for the community."

I would find out later down the line that not everyone would agree with that.

By the beginning of the next week the room was ready for business; there was enough seating for eight people with a few more spare fold ups in the store room if needed. One of the members of the knitting circle had donated a drop leaf dining table which folded up quite neatly so as to not take up too much space but could be used as and when required. I'd offered to pay for any items which had needed to be purchased but Kathleen assured me there was no need; she'd organised a whip round amongst the groups to cover any costs incurred.

The first group to use the room was the book club. The first members started to arrive around one thirty. I'd already met Dave and a few of the others were regular customers or known to me by sight but the rest were strangers. I greeted each one with a smile and directed them to the stairs when they arrived. After a while Dave came down into the cafe with a drinks order. "Have you got a tray I can borrow," he asked, "so I can carry them all up at once."

"Of course," I said, reaching under the counter for one. "Are you sure you can manage them? It will be heavy."

Dave flexed his muscles like a bodybuilder and laughed. "Years of carrying piles of bricks has kept me in good shape."

Olive and I shared the amusement and then she turned to make the coffees while I made the teas.

"I take it you're a builder then" I said, placing three mugs of steaming hot tea on the tray.

"I'm semi-retired now" he said. "I work enough to pay the bills and provide a little extra for luxuries but life's too short not to have some time off to enjoy it."

When he'd taken the tray upstairs Olive sidled up to me and said "You could take a leaf out of his book you know."

I looked at her. "What do you mean?"

"Well you work too hard and all work and no play as they say…"

"Listen who's talking" I said with mock severity. "You're supposed to be retired; you could be at home now with your feet up."

"Yes and going rapidly mad listening to Norman snoring in front of the telly" she said.

"And what would *I* do?" I replied, "sitting at home with no-one to talk to."

"You could take up a hobby," she said, trying to hide a smile.

"So could you," I gave back.

"This *is* my hobby," she said, making us both laugh.

At three o' clock Dave came back down the stairs, carrying a tray of empty mugs, with one of the other members of the club. "Harriet, this is Dorothy," he said, putting the tray down on the counter. "She's come to help me because we'll need two trays for this order."

He handed me a piece of paper with a list of drinks and cakes written on it.

"You mean to tell me that a strong man like you can't manage a tray in each hand" I said quite innocently.

"Of course I could" he answered with a grin "but Dorothy needed to stretch her legs. Didn't you Dot?"

Dorothy laughed. "Whatever you say, Dave."

It was after four and Olive had gone home when the book club broke up. They came down one by one, bringing their empty mugs and plates. Dave was last to appear with the two trays and the last of the crockery.

"Pop them on the counter" I said; "I'll put them in the dishwasher in a minute."

Dave looked round the room; there was only one table still occupied.

"Are you ready for closing?" he asked.

"Not yet, I usually close about five o'clock unless there's no customers in."

"I've time for another coffee then?"

"Yes, take a seat and I'll bring it over."

When I placed the mug in front of him he looked up from the book he was reading.

"Was everything okay for you upstairs?" I asked.

"Perfect" he said, "much more comfortable than the village hall. I don't think anyone wanted to go home.

"That's good. Is that what the club's reading at the moment?" I asked, pointing to the book he had open on the table.

"Yes. To be honest I'm finding it a bit heavy going; it was Kevin's choice and not my usual thing."

"What do you usually read?"

He smiled. "I have quite an eclectic taste in reading matter but don't laugh, my favourite genre is Westerns."

"Why would I laugh?" I said, trying not to do so.

"Most people do but when I was a small boy my dad was cowboy mad; he loved watching them on telly so myself and my older brother grew up with them. My brother always wanted to play cowboys and indians and of course I always had to be the indian or the baddie in the black hat. The only exception was when he was the Lone Ranger and I was allowed to be Tonto."

"Still the Indian though" I said, laughing.

He nodded and laughed along with me.

"Are you a reader?" he asked when we'd stopped.

"When I get the chance but nothing heavy; just a bit of escapism."

"That's the best sort," he said.

The other remaining customers got up to leave and called "Thank you, bye."

Dave pulled a face. "I'd better drink up so you can close."

"No rush" I said. "I need to put the dishwasher on and do some last minute cleaning up."

By the time I'd finished he was ready to leave. "Thanks, Harriet," he said. "I'll see you next week."

Chapter Three

The next morning not long after I'd opened up, my first customer arrived. It was a lady I didn't recognise but I greeted her with a smile. "Good Morning" I said, "if you'd like to take a seat I'll be over in a moment to take your order."

"Are you Harriet Jones?" she demanded, not moving from where she stood.

"Yes" I said, a little taken aback by her abrupt manner. "How can I help you?"

"You can stop poaching my groups for a start!"

"Pardon" I said, "I don't know what you mean, which groups?"

She gave a snort. "Don't give me that. I know what you're up to."

"I really don't. I…"

"My name is Adele Kenyon" she shouted "and I'm chairwoman of the village hall committee."

The penny began slowly to drop. "Why don't you take a seat Mrs Kenyon; I'll pour us a coffee and we can have a chat."

"I don't want anything from you, other than a promise that you'll close your upstairs room to the groups that have started to use them."

She was really starting to irritate me and I could feel the anger starting to boil in my chest. "I'm afraid I'm not prepared to do that" I stated.

She pointed her finger in my face. "People like you make me sick," she spat. "You're stealing revenue from the hall without which it might have to close, depriving the whole community of its use but why should you care? You're not from around here, you're an outsider; you'll make your money out of us and then scuttle off back to where you came from and the sooner that happens the better!"

With that she turned on her heel and marched out of the shop, slamming the door behind her. I stood, numb with shock and on the verge of angry tears. Luckily Olive arrived at that moment. As soon as she walked through the door she could tell something was wrong; my face must have said it all. "Are you alright Harriet, I've just bumped into that battleaxe Adele Kenyon. Quite literally actually; she nearly knocked me over. Has she upset you?"

Despite my determination not to cry, the tears started to roll down my cheeks.

"Oh my dear" said Olive as she came and took me into her arms.

When my tears had dried enough to let me speak I told her what had just happened and the hurtful things Adele Kenyon had said to me.

"Oo I could strangle the dragon," she said. "She doesn't know what she's talking about; you're the kindest, most generous and community spirited person I've ever known."

"I'm only glad there were no customers in at the time to hear it," I said with a sniff.

"She wouldn't have dared speak to you like that if there had been. People around here know what you're like and love you for it. Wait until they find out."

I was horrified at the prospect. "No Olive, don't tell anyone; I couldn't bear it."

Olive pursed her lips as if she was going to argue but then thought the better of it.

"Okay if you insist but I'm going to tell Dave Kenyon next week when he comes to the book club."

"Dave Kenyon? Is he her husband?" I was shocked.

"No, her brother-in-law. She's married to his brother, poor soul. She'll probably send him to an early grave."

"Oh Olive, that's unkind."

She rolled her eyes. "There you are; see what I mean? The woman has just torn you to shreds and now you're feeling sorry for her."

I had to smile. She was right of course but that was me.

The door opened and our first 'real' customers seated themselves at their favourite table by the window.

"Good morning Harriet and Olive" called the Yardley sisters. "Can we have our usual please?"

"Coming up ladies," said Olive, squeezing my hand before going off to put two tea cakes under the grill.

Watching normality, calmed me down and took my mind off previous events.

The groups settled in nicely and I enjoyed having them on the premises. It wasn't just the extra custom, it was meeting new people some of whom often stayed on after their group had finished for extra refreshments and a chat. Dave stayed again after the book club but this time the cafe was empty and he asked me to join him for a coffee; he even offered to pay for them.

"Don't be daft," I said, "these are on the house."

I made the coffees and took them over to the table he'd chosen. He let me settle in opposite him before he spoke. "I believe you've had a visit from my sister-in-law."

I pulled a face at the memory. "Yes I did, who told you? Olive?"

"She mentioned it but I already knew, my brother told me. He was at home when she got back."

I was tempted to give him the full story of what had happened because I was certain he'd only been told *her* side but I held my tongue. I didn't know him very well and didn't want to upset myself reliving the episode. Instead I said "At first I thought she was your wife."

He put up his hands in mock dismay. "Spare me that please."

We both laughed and he continued. "No, it was my brother who was brave enough to marry her."

"I feel sorry for him," I said.

He shook his head. "He's happy enough; he knew what she was like before he married her and actually she's not that bad when you get to know her."

"I don't think I want to get to know her, thank you."

"That's a shame," he said, "because I think the two of you would get along."

"I very much doubt it." I said taking a sip from my coffee to hide my growing irritation.

"Honestly, I mean it. You are both very passionate about things that are important to you. Yours is the tearoom and hers is the village hall."

"But I would never shout at someone and insult them in the way she did me" I retorted, forgetting my promise to myself to keep silent.

"Perhaps not, I agree but her bark is much worse than her bite as the saying goes. It's just that she barks a lot and very loudly."

His attempt at humour soothed my rising temper enough to want to put the matter to rest. "Well it's in the past now" I said "and I'm not one to bear a grudge; I'd rather forget the whole thing."

He handed me a piece of paper. "This is her address and phone number. Why don't you pop round and see her sometime and clear the air."

I took the paper and put it in my apron pocket without looking at it. "I might not bear a grudge but I don't think I'll be dropping in for tea and biscuits any time soon."

He smiled and drank the last of his coffee. "Never mind," he said, "you might feel different in a day or two."

I gave him a look that said 'and perhaps not'.

"I'm sorry, I have to dash," he said as he got up to leave. "I'm off to see a potential customer about a job and he needs to be somewhere else at five thirty. I'll see you next week and thanks for the coffee."

I watched him leave with a sinking sensation in my chest. I wondered if he was disappointed in me and my attitude towards Adele and that was the real reason he'd left so quickly. I also wondered why it mattered so much to me.

Chapter Four

The next morning at work I told Olive about my chat with Dave and how it had made me feel. She looked me straight in the eye and said "Do you like him, Harriet?"

"What do you mean? Yes I like him but only in the same way I like my other customers. Well most of them."

"Mm" she said. "I think you might like him a little differently."

"You make me sound like a schoolgirl with a crush," I said.

She simply looked at me and smiled which irritated me.

"I don't like him like that!" I said it more sharply than I intended.

"You could have fooled me" she said and then darted into the kitchen before I could reply.

She was saved from any retribution by the arrival of the ladies from the knitting circle. Unlike the members of the book club they each bought their drinks as they came in and took them upstairs with them. The last one to arrive was Kathleen Thomas sporting a royal blue tote bag decorated with multi-coloured flowers; the ends of her knitting needles were poking out of the top. "I like your bag, Kathleen" I said, "is it new?"

"It's lovely isn't it?" she said showing it off; "I bought it from the charity shop in Inglesby.

"I think you keep that charity shop going" I said with a smile. "You must be their best customer."

"That's what Fred says but I love charity shops" she said; "you can pick up some real bargains and I do love a bargain."

"It's a pity we don't have one in Underwood" I said.

"I know," said Kathleen. "The one in Inglesby is always busy and attracts tourists as well as locals; it must make lots of funds for the charity it supports."

I placed her latte on the counter and she paid me before going upstairs. "See you at breaktime" she called.

When Olive felt safe to emerge from the kitchen she found me deep in thought.

"By the heck, Harriet, I can almost hear the cogs turning.",

"Pardon?" I said, bringing my head back into the room.

"You look as though you're trying to solve a puzzle but can't quite work it out."

"In a way you're right" I said.

I realised I was still holding the coins that Kathleen had given me for her drink and rang them into the till while Olive waited patiently for an explanation.

"I was thinking that it's a shame there's no charity shop in Underwood; it would be a good fundraiser for some organisation. Kathleen Thomas reckons the one in Inglesby does a roaring trade."

"It does" said Olive, "especially when there are tourists about. My friend Zoe volunteers there and she says they're always busy."

"Do you know if there are any empty shops in Underwood at present?" I asked.

"I don't think there is," replied Olive after giving it some thought, "but I noticed the gift shop next to the butchers is having a closing down sale so there might be one soon."

"D'you mind if I nip out for a moment?" I said; "I'll be back before the knitters come down for their elevenses."

Before she could reply I'd taken off my apron, hung it up in the kitchen and pulled on my jacket. "I won't be long," I said as I breezed past her.

As I walked towards the butchers I could see the brightly coloured notice in the window of the shop next door. Olive had been right. The bell over the door tinkled as I opened it and walked into the shop: Mrs Phillips, the proprietor, was behind the counter and greeted me with a smile.

"Good Morning Harriet, I don't see you in here very often."

I felt a stab of guilt. "I know, I'm sorry about that; is business not good?"

She gave me an apologetic look. "I'm sorry, I didn't mean it like that; it's lovely to see you and business is fine. Why do you ask?"

"Because I saw the sign for the closing down sale."

She pulled a wry face. "I'm afraid it's a physical rather than a financial matter."

"Oh I see."

Since Michael, my husband, passed away I'm finding it increasingly difficult to manage on my own; my joints are giving in to old age I'm afraid."

"Have you found a buyer for the business?"

"Not yet; in fact I haven't actually put it on the market yet because I'm in a bit of a quandary. I own the building and I live in the flat upstairs; ideally I would like someone to rent the shop, otherwise I'll have to move out."

"But if your joints are giving you trouble" I said, "wouldn't you be better in a bungalow?"

She nodded. "I know that's what I'm heading for but I'm not ready for such an upheaval at the moment. Giving up the shop is difficult enough."

"I think I may be able to help you to get what you want but I need to speak to someone else first."

Her face lit up. "That would be fantastic, what do you have in mind?"

I briefly outlined my idea and she beamed from ear to ear. "That sounds like a brilliant idea."

I put my finger over my lips. "Mum's the word until I've approached the third party."

Mrs Phillips mimed pulling a zip across her lips.

As soon as I got back to the tearoom I told Olive where I'd been and why; partly because I needed a favour but mainly because she'd have made my life a misery until I did.

Chapter Five

My stomach was churning as I pulled up outside the house. I felt like I was back at school having been summoned to the headmistresses office to account for some misdemeanour or other. Before I turned off the engine I took the scrap of paper out of my pocket; yes, this was the correct address. Taking my courage in both hands I took the key out of the ignition and dragged myself out of the car.

I looked at the semi- detached, two storey cottage; the morning sun was bouncing off the highly polished windows set in the typical Lakeland grey stone. I'd imagined my nemesis living in something much more grand; picturing her in my mind's eye as a lady of the manor, lording it over her minions; she certainly acted the part. The building I was looking at suggested differently. The presently dormant hanging baskets and the tidily pruned shrubs by the front door along with the neatly tied back curtains hanging at the windows could have belonged to anyone in the village.

Adele must have seen me coming up the path because as I raised my hand to lift the brass knocker, it was taken out of my reach by the door being snatched open. I heard the voice before I saw the face. "If you've come for an apology then you're wasting your time."

I took a deep breath to control my irritation. "No Mrs Kenyon, I haven't come for or with an apology. I've come with a suggestion if you'll hear me out."

She waited a moment as she came to a decision but then curiosity must have got the better of her. "You'd better come in then."

I'd had friendlier invitations but she stood to one side to let me pass and after closing the door led me into the living room. She gestured towards the two seater couch under the window and I took this as an indication that I should take a seat. She sat opposite me in one of the two matching armchairs. "Well" she said, "what is this suggestion you want me to listen to?"

Once again I took a deep breath. "Although I don't apologise for letting the groups use my upstairs room, I do see your point about needing funds for the village hall."

Her expression seemed to lose some of its ferocity. "Go on," she said.

"I think we should open a charity shop in the village with all the profits going towards the upkeep of the village hall." I could sense the list of objections forming on her lips so I quickly went on. "Please hear me out before you give an opinion."

"Very well," she said, "carry on."

"One of my customers was telling me about the charity shop in Inglesby and how well it does, especially in high season when the tourists come in to browse and that is what gave me the idea."

"But I don't think there are any empty shops in Underwood at the moment."

"There aren't at present but Clara Phillips who owns the gift shop is hoping to retire in the new year and is looking for a tenant to take the premises over."

She still seemed sceptical. "I'm not a businesswoman, Mrs Jones, and I wouldn't have the first idea about how to get this venture up and running."

"But I *am* a businesswoman, Mrs Kenyon, and I could help with that."

"Would we be able to afford the rent? I'm sure Clara would need us to pay some."

"Of course and once the shop is up and running I'm sure the income would cover our outgoings and make a profit. It seems to work well for other charities."

She leaned forward in her chair which told me I'd secured her interest. "But how would we pay the rent until then?"

"I've had an idea about that as well" I said, her waning hostility allowing me to start to relax. "The premises will only be available from January which gives us three months to do some fundraising."

"Wait a minute" she said, "this calls for refreshments; give me a minute while I put the kettle on."

The complete change in her manner took me by surprise but I began to feel that unless she was planning to put arsenic in my tea, we had at least formed some sort of truce.

Once we were settled again with coffee and biscuits I carried on where I'd left off. "I'm sure your committee will have lots of experience of fundraising but I have at least one suggestion."

Again she asked me to wait while she got a notepad and pen from the cupboard in the corner. "My memory isn't as good as it used to be so I write everything down these days but go on I'm ready."

"I suggest we hold a table top sale in the village hall. We could charge ten pounds per table; if anyone wants to donate the profits from their stall to the fund then they could have one for free. If you set aside an area for refreshments I would donate some cakes and help out if I can."

She stopped writing and looked at me with a half smile on her face. "Won't that be in competition with your tearoom?"

I smiled back. "I'm sure my business can stand it; I won't go bankrupt."

I was rewarded with an even bigger smile. "I think this is a splendid idea, Mrs Jones, but of course I'll have to run it past the rest of the committee; it isn't my decision alone."

"Of course" I said, not believing for a minute that she couldn't get her own way with the committee. "Please call me Harriet."

"And I'm Adele," she said.

She stood and offered me her hand to shake as if we were meeting for the first time. "I'll be in touch," she said.

Olive was waiting patiently for me when I got back to the 'Bun'. She had come in early to open up for me and was eager to know how I'd got on; she did, however, manage to wait until I'd taken my coat off to ask "Well, how did it go?"

"Really well," I said and then went through all that had been said during my visit.

"So when will we know what's going to happen?" she asked.

"Adele is hoping to call a special meeting of the hall committee tomorrow afternoon and she'll let me know the outcome as soon as she can."

Olive gave a cheeky grin. "Oh it's 'Adele' now is it? You'll soon be bosom buddies, I can tell."

"I wouldn't go that far," I said with a smile, "but at least I don't think she sees me as the enemy any more."

It was late afternoon the following day and Olive was just going home when Adele Kenyon met her in the shop doorway. "Have you come to talk to Harriet?" I heard Olive ask.

"Yes if she's available".

We still had some customers waiting to be served so Olive turned to me and said "I can stay on a bit longer if you want to sit and chat to Mrs. Kenyon."

"Thanks Olive, that would be great if you don't mind."

She quickly went back into the kitchen to take her coat off and then I led Adele to an empty table in the corner where we could talk undisturbed. As soon as she had a minute Olive brought us a pot of tea and two cups.

"Well, how did it go?" I asked, reminding myself of Olive the previous day.

Adele smiled as she poured the tea into the cups. "They were all in agreement with it," she said. "One or two were a bit sceptical at first but I managed to persuade them."

I bet you did, I thought to myself with amusement.

"The upshot is, Harriet, is that they'd like me to set up a separate fund-raising committee which will eventually be responsible for the running of the shop."

"That's brilliant" I said, adding my own milk to my tea.

"I'm glad you think so," said Adele, "because we'd like you to be part of it. We feel you'd be a great asset with your business experience."

I could feel myself walking into a trap. "That's very flattering, Adele, but the tearoom takes up so much of my time…"

She put up her hand to stop me mid-sentence. "I understand how busy you must be and there will be lots of people with more time on their hands who will be willing to give practical help, especially when the shop opens but it's your ideas and organisation skills that we need."

Against my better judgement I was softening. "What would you need me to do?"

Her face lit up into a broad grin as she realised she was winning me over. "I'm proposing to hold a meeting in the village hall on Monday evening for anyone who is interested; would you be able to attend?"

"Yes I'm sure I can manage that."

"Good. After that the fundraising committee will meet separately, when needed, to organise events."

I opened my mouth to speak but she stopped me again. "I promise you it won't be every week, especially after the initial push to raise money to get the shop up and running. What d'you say? Are you in?"

"Yes," I said. "I'll do anything I can to help and I'll start by visiting Mrs Phillips and bringing her up to date."

"Splendid" said Adele, standing up. "Now I must be off, Brian will be home soon and wanting his tea."

I walked with her to the door and opened it for her.

"Until Monday then?" she said.

"Yes, I'll see you then."

I didn't need to tell Olive what had been discussed because she'd been standing behind the counter with her bat ears flapping. "Be careful, Harriet," she said when I'd closed the door. "You don't want to take on too much."

"I will," I said.

"You will what? Be careful or take on too much?"

I didn't reply but I think we both knew the answer.

I decided to call on Clara Phillips before I went home. Her premises were at the end of a block so unlike that over the Toasted Bun her flat had a separate entrance at the side of the building. I pushed the buzzer on the intercom and after a few minutes I heard Mrs Phillip's voice through the speaker. "Hello, who's there?"

"It's Harriet Jones, Mrs Phillips; may I come up and have a quick word?"

"Yes of course" she said and I heard the click as she unlocked the door.

When I got to the top of the stairs Mrs Phillips was waiting for me. "Come in Harriet," she said, "it's lovely to see you."

She led me into the sitting room which was prettily furnished with a rose pink velvet three piece suite arranged around the half-moon rug in front of the fireplace. In the corner by the window stood a beautifully ornate jardiniere which held a magnificent india rubber plant with leaves that gleamed like highly polished green leather.

I politely refused a cup of tea as I was eager to get home but we sat and chatted for a while and I told her of the developments in my plan.

"That's wonderful" she said and once the charity shop is open I'll be able to volunteer a few hours a week because it's meeting the customers that I'll miss the most."

"Of course we'll pay you a fair rent," I said; "someone will be in touch with you to discuss it."

She nodded her head and smiled. "I won't be too demanding. We'll be able to come to an arrangement that suits everyone I'm sure."

Chapter Six

I decided it would be a waste of time and petrol to go home after work on Monday and then come back for the meeting at seven o clock; it made better sense to have something to eat in the tearoom. The upstairs room was quite homely since the groups had made it their own so I could bring my book and relax in one of the armchairs for an hour or so but when Olive learned of my plans she wouldn't hear of it and insisted I went home with her for something to eat.

"Norman will have something ready for us when we get home and then we can go to the meeting together." she said.

I pretended to be surprised. "I didn't know you intended to go to the meeting."

She shrugged. "It's open to anyone in the village who might be interested and I am."

I couldn't help but smile. "Is this an interest in helping or or just plain nosiness?"

She gave me a look of mock horror and then laughed. "You know me too well, Harriet Jones."

I gave her a hug. "I wouldn't have you any other way but I thought Monday was your soap opera night."

"It is but Norman will record them for me and I'm much more interested in what's going on on my own doorstep than in some fictional suburb of London or Manchester."

I was half convinced until she added "And someone has to make sure you don't take too much on."

Norman is a really good cook and it was a lovely change for me to enjoy a home cooked meal I hadn't prepared myself. This was the first time since my one-time lodger, Rose, had left me at Easter.

"It's nothing fancy ,Harriet," he said as he took the casserole out of the oven and set it on a mat in the middle of the dining table already laden with dishes of carrot and swede, cauliflower and buttery mashed potatoes.

"It smells divine, Norman, thank you for inviting me."

"It's always a pleasure, Harriet, now help yourself."

The food tasted as good as it looked and smelled and I ate heartily. In fact I was beginning to think I'd overindulged when after clearing the plates Norman returned from the kitchen carrying a large trifle. "I hope you've left room for pudding," he said. So did I.

"Do you eat like that every evening?" I asked Olive as we walked arm in arm towards the village hall.

"You must be joking," she said, "I'd be as fat as a pig in no time. All that was for your benefit."

"Well that was very kind of him," I said.

"He likes to entertain and we don't do it very often these days."

"Y'know if you ever feel like retiring" I said with my tongue firmly in my cheek, "I would welcome his services at the 'Toasted Bun'".

"Watch it!" she said, nipping my arm.

"Ouch! That hurt!"

"It was meant to," she said.

The hall was nearly half full when we arrived. Adele was on the stage arranging chairs behind a long table; when she spotted Olive and I, she stopped what she was doing and came over to greet us. "Good evening ladies," she said. "Harriet, I would like you to join us on the stage if that's okay with you."

It wasn't: I couldn't think of anything further away from my comfort zone.

"If you don't mind, Adele, I'd rather sit in the body of the hall with Olive."

She looked disappointed. "But this was your idea."

"I know and I'll help all I can but I'm more comfortable being a warrior than a chief."

She still looked unhappy with my decision but said "Well, if you're sure but you must sit in the front row."

The front row was already full but Adele went straight to the couple in the end seats and asked them politely but firmly to move. I could feel myself going hot with embarrassment and started to protest but the couple seemed to know their place and did as they were told. I muttered an apology as they passed us.

At 7 o'clock on the dot Adele banged a small wooden gavel on the table and brought the meeting to order. She took a seat on the middle one of three chairs behind the table. On her right sat the local vicar, a young man in his thirties whom I knew by sight but had never met and on her left sat a stern looking middle aged woman in a woollen two piece suit and a matching felt hat. Adele introduced them even though I was probably the only person in the room who didn't know Reverend Karl Quayle and Mrs Wanda Barraclough, who was to take down the minutes.

Adele opened the meeting by outlining the financial needs of running the village hall and the proposed fundraising to meet those needs before inviting questions and comments from the floor. There were more of the latter than the former but Adele was more than capable of dealing with both.

Clara Phillips was in the audience and was happy to add her support for the proposed charity shop. A member of the audience raised their hand to ask how much rent she would charge but before Clara could answer Adele jumped in to state that no figure had been agreed as yet but it was in the hands of the fundraising committee. She then announced that anyone interested in joining the fundraising committee should give their names to the secretary at the end of the meeting.

"Of course, Mrs Harriet Jones," she said "who came up with the idea of the charity shop has already volunteered."

Olive whispered in my ear. "Volunteered or press ganged?"

I gave a wry smile but was saved from answering by Adele continuing to speak.

"If there are no more questions or comments I will close the meeting and invite you all to join us for refreshments prepared by the ladies of the catering committee."

There was an outbreak of chatter and a general movement to the back of the hall where tables had been set out with a range of small cakes and biscuits surrounding a tea urn and large coffee pot. Olive and I decided to let the queue die down before we joined everyone else.

"I certainly don't want a piece of cake," I said, "I'm still stuffed from Norman's banquet."

"Me too," said Olive "but I wouldn't mind a cuppa."

"Sorry to interrupt ladies" said a voice at my side. I turned to see Reverend Quayle beaming back at me with his hand held out. "I believe you're Mrs Jones; I've heard so much about you but I don't believe we've actually met."

Feeling at a disadvantage looking up at him I stood up before shaking the proffered hand.

"No I'm afraid I'm not much of a churchgoer, vicar, and I'm usually working Sundays."

"I completely understand," he said with a smile, "Sunday is my busy day as well."

I turned to introduce him to Olive but she'd vanished so I invited Reverend Quayle to sit with me but he shook his head. "Perhaps we can chat another time" he said; "I need to get home. Monday is officially my day off but no-one refuses a summons from Adele."

He said this with a straight face but then began to laugh. I joined in and said "I sort of know what you mean."

When he left me I looked round for Olive and finally spotted her, deep in conversation with the stern Mrs Barraclough although her manner appeared to be much more jovial now. Olive saw me looking and beckoned me over.

"Harriet, I want you to meet Wanda Barraclough, she and I have been friends for a long time."

"Pleased to meet you Harriet" said Wanda, "I may call you Harriet?"

"Yes of course" I said, completing my second handshake of the evening.

"Then please call me Wanda and before you ask I believe I was named after some siren of the silver screen my mother was a big fan of."

She was smiling and I laughed. "I wasn't going to but I expect a lot of people do."

"All the time" she said, "so I've developed the habit of explaining things to get it out of the way."

Even though the sternness had disappeared I got the impression that Wanda was a very forthright person who didn't hesitate to speak her mind and I wondered how she and Adele Kenyon got along together.

Olive cut through my thoughts. "Wanda will be part of the fundraising committee so you'll see her fairly often."

"Not too often I hope, Wanda. No offence but Adele promised me it wouldn't take up too much of my time."

Wanda placed her hand on my arm. "No offence taken my dear but I'm afraid Adele has you in her clutches now and she's a woman who's difficult to say no to."

I inwardly groaned and hoped I didn't live to regret this.

Before we left I went over to say goodbye to Adele.

"Thanks for coming Harriet, I'll be in touch to let you know when the first meeting is."

I'd left my car at Olive's and on the way back I said "Wanda seems a nice person but she seemed ever so stern when she walked onto the stage."

"I think she'd had words with Adele Kenyon before the meeting started," said Olive "and you're right she is a nice person but you wouldn't want to cross her."

"I expect she and Adele have *words* quite often" I remarked.

"So do I" said Olive "and I'm looking forward to you reporting back to me after your committee meetings."

I approached my tasks with an extra spring in my step the following morning which wasn't lost on Olive when she arrived for work.

"You're very cheery this morning" she said as she hung up her coat.

"Well it's a lovely day and I'm in a happy mood."

"And it's nothing to do with it being Tuesday."

"Why would that make a difference?" I asked innocently.

She came out of the kitchen, tying her apron strings behind her back. "Because it's book club day and you quite like one of the members if I recall correctly."

I couldn't look her in the eye so I concentrated on filling the coffee machine with fresh beans. "I've told you, he's just another customer."

"You know who I mean then."

I turned to face her, meaning to firmly disabuse her of this notion she'd developed but the wide grin on her face softened my words. "Yes, I do know who you mean and *yes* I do like him; I admit I enjoy his company but I'm not a lovesick teenager. Besides, I expect he's married."

"Divorced" she informed me. "Quite a long time ago in fact."

"Oh" I said and gave her the satisfaction of seeing my involuntary smile.

"I won't tease you any more," she said, becoming more serious, "but perhaps it wouldn't be a bad thing for you to have someone special in your life apart from your children and grandchildren."

"I already have," I said.

"Who?"

"You."

With a sigh of resignation and a shake of her head she went back into the kitchen knowing when she was beaten.

Chapter Seven

Dorothy Green was the first to arrive and waved to me as she made her way through the tables to the stairs.

"I'm a little early," she said, "so I'll wait for the others to arrive and order my drink with them."

We were slap bang in the middle of the lunchtime rush so I was kept too busy to notice the rest of the members arriving in dribs and drabs; I was in the kitchen filling the dishwasher when I heard Olive's voice in the cafe.

"Is someone coming down to help you with the trays, Dorothy?"

"Yes Kevin will be here in a minute."

My ears pricked up as Olive asked "No Dave today?"

"No," said Dorothy. "He's got some work on, so it looks like he won't make it this afternoon."

"I thought he normally made sure he kept Tuesday afternoons free" persisted Olive.

"Normally he does but I think this is a rush job. Kevin could tell you properly, he took the message."

"Oh well, needs must sometimes I suppose."

I carried on with what I was doing not wanting Olive to see my disappointment because it would only strengthen her argument but I couldn't deny how my heart had sunk when I heard their conversation. You're just being stupid anyway I told myself; he's simply another customer whom you like chatting to. He's no different from the Yardley sisters but yet

I knew that wasn't quite true and something was bothering me.

Olive knew I must have heard her conversation with Dorothy but tactfully didn't mention it when I rejoined her at the counter; in fact I was the one to bring up the subject.

"Do you think Dave Kenyon is avoiding me?"

Olive looked at me in genuine surprise. "Why on earth would he do that?"

"I was pretty insulting about Adele the last time we spoke; perhaps he was offended."

Olive laughed. "If he was offended by any of the bad things said about Adele in his presence he'd be avoiding most of the village."

"I wanted to tell him that I'd taken his advice and gone to see her and that we'd made up."

"He might know already," said Olive. "He and his brother are quite close I believe and Brian probably uses him quite often as a sympathetic ear, so it's possible he's told him."

"Hm" I said, not totally convinced. "Perhaps you're right."

Olive frowned. "I know I teased you before, Harriet, but perhaps you do like Dave a little more than you're even admitting to yourself."

"I'm just being stupid" I said, "I've only met the man a couple of times and yes I do enjoy his company but it doesn't mean he enjoys mine."

I turned away from the sympathy that washed over my friend's face as for once she was lost for words. I could feel the tears pricking behind my eyes which made me cross with myself for being so foolish. I knew Olive wanted to comfort me but she knew me well enough to know that I would pull myself together more easily if I was left alone so she didn't follow me when I went back into the kitchen and took my frustration out on cleaning the oven. It worked a treat and by the time the book club members left I was back to my old self again. I was grateful to Olive for holding the fort so rewarded her with an early finish.

"We've no customers" I said, "so you get off home and I'll finish cleaning up and not be long behind you."

After she'd gone I went to the front door to lock up but as I was turning the 'closed' sign round a body appeared in the doorway making me jump.

I recognised the voice before I clearly saw the face. "Oh am I too late?"

I kept the closed sign on but unlocked the door to let him in.

"I'm sorry" he said, as I stood to one side to let him pass. "There was an accident on the motorway; a lorry had spilled its load and I've been stuck in traffic. I knew I'd miss the book club but I thought I might be in time to snatch a coffee before you closed."

"Well, I was closing a little early because we had no customers but take a seat and I'll make you a drink."

"Have you got any food left? I'm famished."

"I'm sure I can find you something" I said with a chuckle, "I don't want you dropping from starvation on my doorstep; it wouldn't be good for business."

We hadn't much left but I made him a sandwich with the chicken I'd intended to take home for my supper and there was a slice of victoria sponge in the fridge. When I placed it on the table in front of him his eyes lit up with pleasure.

"That's great Harriet, will you join me."

I made two cups of coffee and sat down with him. He almost inhaled the food before he said "That's filled a corner."

"You weren't kidding when you said you were famished" I said with a laugh.

"I'd had nothing since breakfast; I finished the job at lunchtime and wanted to get straight off to make it to the book club. My idea was to have some lunch here but the best laid plans as they say."

"So have you finished the job?" I asked, taking a sip of my coffee.

"Yes, I worked through the weekend so I'm going to treat myself to a couple of days off."

"I don't blame you," I said. "What are you going to do with your time off then?"

"Sleep mainly," he said laughing, "but I might do a spot of fishing; I'll give my brother a ring and see if he can get away to join me."

"Speaking of your brother, I've made friends with Adele."

"Really?" he said with a big smile. "How did that come about?"

I sighed. "It's a long story."

He interrupted before I could elaborate. "I'll tell you what, why don't we go over to the pub for a meal and a drink. Then, you can tell me the story, no matter how long it is."

I wasn't expecting that and was momentarily lost for words so he went on. "The food you brought me was very welcome but it hardly touched the sides and it will save you cooking when you get home.

"Well…"

"Besides," he said, "I'm intrigued to hear how you managed to make up with the formidable Adele."

I let myself be persuaded. "Okay you've won me over; just give me a minute to finish up here."

The Bull was the only pub in the village but it served excellent food; as it was early in the evening and a Tuesday we were able to get a table quite easily. Once we were settled and we'd ordered our food I told my story.

"I told you she wasn't all bad" said Dave, "I'm pleased you've made friends with her."

"I wouldn't actually say we were friends but I think we can get along without too much trouble."

"I'm sure you can but be careful that she doesn't ask too much of you; she's so passionate about her causes and she thinks everyone feels the same and she has a lot more time on her hands than you do."

"Are you speaking from experience?"

He laughed. "A little but it's my brother who gets dragged into all sorts of things and not always willingly."

At this point our meals arrived and demanded our full attention but afterwards we chatted like old friends until the landlord called last orders.

"Gosh" I said, "is that the time?" I'd better be going - we can't all have the luxury of a lie in tomorrow morning."

"No I suppose not" he said "but I'll walk you back to your car; I'm parked behind you anyway."

The walk was far too short but when we reached the cars I said "Thanks for this evening Dave, I've really enjoyed myself but I wish you'd let me go halves with the bill."

"No, it was my treat and I've really enjoyed it as well. Perhaps we can do it again sometime."

"I'd like that," I said.

He kissed me lightly on the cheek. "Goodnight Harriet, I'll see you soon."

He stood and watched as I drove away before getting into his own car. I hardly remember driving home as I went over the events of the evening. I'd enjoyed myself more than I had for a long time and forgave myself for being a middle aged woman acting like a teenager.

When I got home the light was flashing on my answering machine but I hung up my coat and changed into my slippers before I listened to the message.

"Hi Mum, it's me Naiomi, can you give me a ring when you get in?"

I looked at the clock. It was too late to ring her now, she'd most likely have gone to bed. I decided to leave it until the morning; I'd be able to catch her before she went to work.

Chapter Eight

Early next morning I was woken by the phone ringing in the living room but before I could get to it, it had stopped. There was a message.

"Hi Mum, it's me again. I tried you last night but you must have missed my message. Please give me a call when you can."

I immediately rang back.

"Hello love, is something wrong?"

"Have you heard from Vin?" she asked.

"No. why?"

I heard her sigh. "That's typical of my brother. I told him to ring you; he's been made redundant."

"Oh no."

"Yes and it's causing trouble between him and Elaine; they're arguing all the time."

It was on the tip of my tongue to say 'what's new?' but I didn't. Instead I said "I'll give him a ring later on when Elaine's at work, he'll be able to talk more freely."

"I'm sorry to bother you with this Mum but I'm worried about him."

"That's fine love, I'll talk to him."

I put the receiver down and sat on the couch to collect my thoughts. My son, Vincent, was an electrician by trade but he could turn his hand to lots of things; his dad had been the same. His partner, Elaine, had two young boys from a previous marriage and Vincent had moved in with them shortly before I moved to Underwood. His and Elaine's relationship had always been quite volatile but they seemed to thrive on this. I had made a promise to myself a long time ago never to interfere in my children's relationships and decisions but I was still his mother and I needed to know that my son was okay.

I went to work with a heavy heart. I loved my life in the Lake District but I often missed my children and grandchildren. I had always comforted myself in that they were also happy with *their* lives but now I felt the distance between us and all I wanted to do was speak to my son and help him if I could.

I put on a brave face when Olive came in because I wasn't ready to talk about it to anyone. My cause was helped by the fact that she and Norman had had an argument before she came out and she was too busy venting her anger at him to notice any change in me.

The knitters arrived and took their refreshments upstairs so I busied myself in the kitchen preparing sandwiches for lunch. I was deep in my own thoughts when Olive popped her head round the door; she was smiling.

"Harriet, you have a visitor."

I'm embarrassed to say my heart gave a little leap at the thought it would be Dave but it wasn't.

"Hiya Mum."

I stopped in my tracks. "Vincent!"

I went to greet him and took him in my arms for a tight bear hug. When I released him I looked up and saw that the smile on his lips wasn't mirrored in his eyes.

"Why don't you sit down and I'll make us both a drink. Are you hungry?"

"No, I stopped off at a motorway services for breakfast but a coffee would be great."

For once Olive kept a lid on her questions but I could tell she was curious.

"Do you mind if I take ten minutes?" I asked.

"Not at all, it probably won't get busy until the knitters come down."

"Thanks" I said with a look that said 'I'll tell you later'.

I sat across the table from my son and waited for him to say something but I could tell he was struggling so I spoke first.

"I was going to ring you later actually."

He raised his eyebrows. "Really? Why?"

"Don't be annoyed but Naiomi rang me; she said you'd been made redundant."

He gave a sad smile. "I should have known she couldn't keep it to herself."

"She's your big sister; she cares about you."

"I know. I was going to tell you myself but I was hoping I would get another job quickly and wouldn't have to worry you."

"What happened?"

"The firm I was working for went bust so although I was 'technically' made redundant I don't know when I'll see any severance pay."

"How has Elaine taken it?" I asked even though I knew the answer.

"Not well; in fact she's thrown me out."

"What! Because you lost your job through no fault of your own?"

"There's a lot more to it than that, Mum."

I could hear the knitters coming down the stairs and the lunchtime rush was about to begin. "Look." I said, "I'll give you my house key; why don't you go back to mine and I'll be home as soon as I can."

He nodded and I stood up to leave him but he called me back. "Can I stay with you for a bit, Mum?"

I went back and hugged him again. "Oh love, you can stay with me as long as you want to."

I watched him leave the cafe but then I was needed to work so it was a while before I could bring Olive up to date.

"Why don't you get off home?" she said. "I can manage for the rest of the afternoon and I'll cash up and lock up for you."

"If you're sure?"

"Of course I am. I'll ring Norman and ask him to come and help me."

I put my arms around her and kissed her on the cheek. "You're a star, Olive Parker."

"I know," she said with a chuckle.

"I hope you don't mind," said Vincent when I walked through the front door. "I've put my stuff in the spare bedroom."

"That's fine," I said. "Where's your van?"

"I parked it round the back if that's okay."

I nodded. "It's a good job the van was your own and didn't belong to the company."

"I know because Elaine needs the car."

I didn't comment on the fact that he'd paid for it but took my bags into the kitchen. Vincent followed me.

"I've brought something from the cafe for dinner" I said, "did you have any lunch?"

"Yes I made a sandwich - there was some ham in the fridge, was that okay?"

"Of course. Shall I put the kettle on and you can tell me what's been going on."

I waited until we were both seated in a comfy chair in the lounge before I prompted him to speak.

"Things haven't been good between me and Elaine for some time. I wanted to get married and have a child of our own. Don't get me wrong I love the boys but…"

"I know what you mean" I said "but I take it Elaine wasn't keen on the idea."

"She turned me down flat; said she didn't want any more children and we didn't need a piece of paper to seal our relationship."

I could see he was really hurting but couldn't find the right words to console him. I waited patiently for him to continue.

"When I lost my job she said she couldn't afford to keep me while I was out of work as she had the boys to think about so I'd better move out."

I had not seen my son cry since he was a small boy but I could see the tears gathering in his eyes.

"When she left for work this morning she told me to be gone by the time she got home."

"Oh son" was all I could say. I had never been Elaine's greatest fan but as long as Vincent had been happy I had made the best of it and I looked on her boys as my own grandsons. I felt the rage rising in me when I considered her thoughtless cruelty but I was wise enough not to give voice to my thoughts.

"I had nowhere else to go," he said. "I suppose Naiomi would have taken me in but she hasn't really got the room."

"You did exactly the right thing in coming here" I said, "you'll always have a home with me."

"Thanks Mum. I can pay my way for now; Elaine always insisted on separate bank accounts so I have some money of my own to tide me over but I'll need to find some work soon."

"I'll put the word out," I said. "You could go self-employed: I'll help you with the paperwork to get set up and I'm sure you'd get plenty of work round here while you decide what you want to do but you're welcome to stay as long as you like."

After we'd eaten, I persuaded him to ring Naiomi while I was washing up. I would have rang her myself but I thought it was better coming from him and he could tell her as much or as little as he wanted her to know.

Chapter Nine

The next morning I was able to release all of my pent up anger by telling Olive the whole story.

"No wonder the lad needed his mum" she said when I'd finished. "I think he's well shut of that one."

"Between us, so do I" I said, "but I wouldn't say that to *him* at the moment. I think it's the boys he'll miss the most, he thinks the world of them.

Olive nodded. "Yes, it's those two I feel the most sorry for; in a way it's the second time they've lost a dad."

"I hadn't thought of that but you're right."

"What's he going to do with himself today?"

"I think he's going fishing."

She rolled her eyes. "Not another one; I'll have to ask Norman to take him to the fishing club."

"Actually that's not a bad idea, Olive, especially if he stays for a while."

"Why don't you put a card in the window advertising his services - as an electrician I mean."

"Olive Parker, that's the second good idea you've had in the space of five minutes" I said.

She breathed on her fingernails and then rubbed them against her shoulder.

"I know," she said, "I'm pure genius."

It was almost lunchtime when Adele Kenyon paid us a visit. There was a queue at the counter which she completely ignored as she pushed her way forward. The lady at the front started to protest but Adele cut her short.

"I'm not here to buy anything. I just want a word with Harriet."

She couldn't have picked a worse time but she came straight to the point.

"Fundraising meeting, tomorrow night, seven o'clock in the village hall. See you there. Bye." Then she was gone.

I realised my mouth was still open, frozen in the act of trying to reply.

"That's you told," said the woman at the front of the queue.

A committee meeting was the last thing I needed at the moment; it meant leaving Vincent on his own again.

"I know he's not a child," I said to Olive later, "but he's really down in the dumps at the moment."

"He'll be fine," she said. "I think there's footie on the telly tomorrow night; I wish I had a committee meeting to go to."

Vincent was fine when I told him about the meeting. "You mustn't put your life on hold because of me or I'll feel I'm in the way."

"You are certainly not that" I said with feeling.

"Good and I think it's a brilliant idea to put a card in the cafe window. With a bit of luck it will get me some work."

I made a point of being early for the meeting as I was sure lateness would not be tolerated by the chairwoman. When I arrived Adele and Wanda were already there. A table had been put up in the body of the hall with chairs surrounding it. Adele was seated at one end and Wanda at the other. I didn't know if this was deliberate to put as much space between them as possible or to allow them to exchange icy glares.

Both women, however, greeted me warmly which left me in a dilemma - do I sit next to Adele or Wanda? The decision was taken from me when Adele said "You sit next to me, Harriet, I'll look after you while it's your first meeting."

I did as I was told but not before I caught Wanda rolling her eyes.

Dorothy Green was next to arrive; I knew her from the book club and without hesitation she took a seat next to Wanda. Next came a young woman I didn't know but she introduced herself as she took the seat between me and Wanda.

"Hello, you must be Harriet. I'm Belinda Quayle; I believe you've already met my husband, Karl."

"Yes" I said, shaking her hand, "on both counts."

It was now five minutes to seven and I was aware of Adele looking at her watch every few seconds. I didn't know who was due to take up the remaining empty chair but I thought they'd better hurry up if they knew what was good for them. On the dot of seven the door opened and in strolled a middle aged woman who was vaguely familiar. I was sure she sometimes came into the cafe but I couldn't recall her name. She washed the rest of us with a beaming smile and then took the seat between Adele and Dorothy. I couldn't rid myself of the notion that she had been standing outside waiting until the last minute to make an appearance.

Clearing her throat in a dramatic manner Adele declared the meeting open and gave a brief recount of the reason for forming the fundraising committee. She then distributed copies of the agenda she had drawn up.

"Item one" said Adele; "we need to decide on a date and time for the table top sale. Have you brought the hall diary Wanda?"

"Of course" said Wanda, producing an A4 hard backed book from her bag. "When were we thinking of?"

"We need time to advertise," said Dorothy "and to give people time to book stalls."

"If we said mid-November" I ventured, "it could double up as a Christmas Fayre."

"Good idea, Harriet," said Belinda. "Crafters could sell items for people to buy as Christmas presents."

Wanda turned the pages of the diary. "What about the second Saturday in November?"

"I'll second that" said the woman opposite.

"Those in favour" said Adele as we all raised our hands.

It was decided that ten a.m. until four p.m. would be a reasonable amount of time for the event. It would give people time to set up and pack away on the day.

"How many tables do we have, Nell?" asked Belinda, addressing the woman opposite me.

"Twenty but we may not need them all."

"We would need some for the refreshment area" I said.

"Oh of course" said Nell. "Are you going to be in charge of the refreshments, Harriet?"

"Yes I will."

"Won't you need to be in the cafe, Harriet?" asked Dorothy.

I'd given the matter some thought before I came to the meeting so I was able to answer straight away. "I've decided I'll close the cafe that day and my staff and I will take care of the refreshments here if that's okay with everyone. I'll even put a note on the door directing people to the hall; it might boost sales on the stalls as well."

"That's very kind of you Harriet," said Wanda, "what type of food were you thinking of doing?"

"I thought of bacon or sausage rolls in the morning and a selection of sandwiches and cakes in the afternoon."

"That sounds perfect," said Belinda. "My mouth's watering at the thought of it."

After that the next item on the agenda was promotion. Adele volunteered to organise the printing of fliers and posters when we'd agreed on the wording. It was decided to charge ten pounds per stall for which the hall would provide a table and two chairs; any other equipment to be supplied by the stallholder.

By the time we came to 'any other business' I was relieved when no-one had any as I was ready for home.

"In that case" announced Adele, "I suggest we meet again at the same time next week for a progress report."

Everyone was in agreement with this so Adele declared the meeting closed.

I put my chair on one of the stacks in the storage area and turned to find Nell behind me. As she put her chair on top of mine she said "May I have a word, Harriet, in private?"

"Of course," I said, feeling intrigued."

We said our goodbyes to the others and then headed for the car park; when we were sure we were out of earshot of everyone, Nell said "I run a local art group and I was wondering if your room was free on a Saturday morning."

"Yes it is."

She hesitated before she continued, "I want to set up a life drawing class but obviously we need somewhere private where we're not overlooked."

"Oh I see. Well, no-one would disturb you up there and you could close the curtains if necessary."

"And you wouldn't mind? You do know what I mean by a 'life' class?"

I laughed. "Of course I do and your model could get changed in the other room."

"That's brilliant" she said, "it's a bit late to organise things for this Saturday but could we start next week?"

"That's absolutely fine" I said but as she turned towards her car I stopped her. "I know your face, Nell, do you come into the cafe?"

"Occasionally" she said, "but I'm often too busy to come into the village; I'm a potter and rent a studio in an outbuilding in one of the local farms."

Recognition came at once. "Of course you are! I bought some coffee mugs and soup bowls from you last year."

"That's right, you did."

"Can I ask you something else?"

"Go ahead."

"Were you waiting outside earlier, so you could walk in at the last minute?"

"Harriet!" she exclaimed, giving me a smile that made her eyes sparkle, "how could you think such a thing?"

Vincent was sprawled on the couch reading a newspaper when I got home but he looked up when I entered the room.

"You look bushed, Mum, sit yourself down and I'll put the kettle on."

"Thanks Vin, can I have a cup of tea please?"

"Coming up" he called from the kitchen.

The steaming brew hit just the right spot. I kicked off my shoes and let the depths of the armchair enfold me.

"If you make up a list of any odd jobs you need doing around the house" he said, settling back on the couch, "I'll take care of them while you're at work tomorrow."

"Aw thanks son, there are one or two I haven't got around to but it's my day off on Saturday so why don't we have a day out, just the two of us?"

"I'd like that Mum."

Chapter Ten

It was lovely to spend some quality time with my son. We'd always had a close relationship but unlike Naiomi, his interests were very different from mine and he'd spent most of his leisure time either playing or watching sport. He'd missed his father a great deal when he passed as Eric had been the one to ferry him around and share in his enthusiasm.

Vincent had never been one to wear his heart on his sleeve and had hidden his grief at his father's death very convincingly to everyone except myself and Naiomi. Only we knew how much he was hurting behind the mask. It was the same now. He might look to all the world that he was coping so well with the break up with Elaine but I knew my son better than that.

We chose a spot on the shore of Lake Windermere to share the picnic I'd prepared. The weather was warm for the time of year so it was perfect for eating *al fresco*. Besides the food, I'd packed a couple of folding deck chairs and a small table. Vincent laughed as he set them up in the shelter of a pile of rocks.

"What are you laughing at?" I said as I lay a cloth on the table.

"I was just thinking how this reminded me of outings we had when I was a kid."

I stood up and brought the memories to mind.

"We had some good times, didn't we Mum? Doing nothing much but enjoying each other's company and the scenery."

"Yes" I said, feeling the tears prick the back of my eyes. "It was your dad who taught you to fish. I remember how delighted you were when he bought you your first rod."

"Remember how I used to chase Naiomi with the maggots?"

"Yes, you cruel boy" I said, my laughter taking the sting out of my words.

Suddenly his face became solemn. "I was looking forward to similar outings with Elaine and the boys but I suppose that won't happen now."

"Have you heard anything from her?" I asked.

He shook his head. "She made the situation perfectly clear when she threw my stuff into the garden in bin bags."

I went over and took him into my arms. "I'm so sorry," I said.

He surrendered to the hug for a few minutes and then broke away. "Perhaps it's for the best in the long run," he admitted. "We wanted such different things out of life and when I couldn't contribute to the household finances…"

I held him at arm's length. "Even so, it was a bit nasty, the way she treated you."

"Don't judge her too harshly, Mum. She was left in such dire straits when her first husband left her that it made financial security very important to her."

"You're too soft," I said.

"I wonder where I get that from," he said.

Dave was early for the book club on Tuesday afternoon. "I've got a free day today, so I thought I'd have some lunch before the meeting."

"The menus are on the table" I said with a smile. "If you'd like to take a seat I'll be over in a few minutes to take your order."

"I don't suppose you'd like to join me?"

I looked around the tea room; most of the tables were occupied as it was our busiest time.

"I'd love to but I can't leave Olive on her own at the moment, however I might have time for a coffee before you go upstairs."

He took a seat and after a few minutes I went over with my pad. About one thirty, custom had slackened a little so after checking with Olive I poured myself a coffee and took it over to Dave's table. He was engrossed in a book but looked up when I sat opposite him.

"Oh good," he said, placing his bookmark in the page. "I'm glad you've got time for a chat."

"Olive will call me if she needs me but she's okay at the moment."

"I noticed the card in the door" he said; "the electrician looking for work, Vincent Jones. Is he any relation to you?"

"Yes, actually he's my son. He's been made redundant and broke up with his partner so he's staying with me for a while."

"I might be able to put some work his way."

"Really? That would be great."

"I've got some refurbishing work starting next week and I'll be needing a sparks."

"Oh Dave, thank you so much, he'll be grateful."

"I could do with having a chat with him."

I had an idea. "Why don't you come back with me when I close up; you could eat with us and then have that chat."

"Sounds like a good plan" he said with a beaming smile. "I never turn down the offer of a free meal."

"Good, I'll give him a ring and tell him you're coming."

When the book club members had all left, the tearoom was empty so I closed up. Dave was in his work van so he followed me home and parked behind me in front of the cottage. I unlocked the door and as we stepped into the living room a waft of something delicious invaded our senses. Vincent was in the kitchen but he popped his head round the living room door when he heard us come in.

"You're a little early, it's not quite ready."

"That's okay," I said, "do you want me to take over?"

"No thanks, I've made a cottage pie and I just need to brown it in the oven; you two sit down and I'll make us all a drink.

"Right Dave," I said, indicating that he took one of the armchairs, "let's do as we're told."

Vincent joined us with the drinks shortly afterwards. "I've set the timer," he said, with a knowing look before I could say anything.

He sat on the couch and came straight to the point. "Mum says you might be able to put some work my way, Dave."

I could see Dave was impressed by his enthusiasm. "Yes, I hope so."

He went on to describe the next project he was involved with and asked Vincent about what experience he had. I only half listened to what they were saying because I knew nothing about the building trade and when the alarm rang out on the oven they were so engrossed in conversation that I decided I'd better dish up. So much for putting the timer on then, I thought. It was only when I called them in to eat that Vincent realised. "Oh I'm sorry, Mum, I was supposed to be doing everything."

"That's alright," I said with a smile, "I don't mind."

Conversation was sparse as we concentrated on the food. "If you're as good an electrician as you are a cook," said Dave, laying his knife and fork on his empty plate, "I'll guarantee you'll get plenty of work."

"I had a good teacher," said Vincent, nodding in my direction "with the cooking, I mean, not the electrics."

"No, it takes me all my time to wire a plug," I said. "Shall we take our coffee into the living room? I'll wash up later."

"No, Mum, I'll take care of that. You go and put your feet up and chat to Dave."

"Again," I said to Dave, "let's do as we're told."

"My, you've trained that lad well," he said when we were once again ensconced in the armchairs."

"To be honest, he didn't need much training; he's always been a good lad. He doesn't deserve to be in the position he is at the moment."

"His partner must have been mad to let him go."

I glanced at the kitchen door which was closed. "I know most mothers don't think any other woman is good enough for their son but I never really took to Elaine. I always felt she was a user."

"I see," he said, frowning.

"Oh I never voiced my opinions about her to Vincent, she was his choice. I always hoped I was wrong but…" I shrugged my shoulders.

"Do they have any children?"

"Not together. Elaine already had twin boys from a previous marriage when Vincent met her. They weren't much more than babies and he's always treated them like his own."

Dave's frown deepened. "He'll be really missing them, I expect."

"Like mad. Much more than he misses Elaine, I think."

I felt that Dave was on the point of saying something else but Vincent came into the room at that moment and we changed the subject. Shortly afterwards Dave got up to take his leave. "Thank you, both of you, for a lovely meal," he said. "I hate to eat and run but I've a stack of paperwork waiting for me at home."

"That's okay," I said; "I'll come to the door with you."

"Thank you," he said. "I'll see you in a couple of days, Vincent, with the details."

Vincent got up and shook his hand. "Thanks so much, Dave, you don't know how much this means to me."

"I think I might," said Dave. "I've been in that position myself."

When we got to the front door, I closed the living room door behind me. "Are you alright Dave?" I asked.

He gave me a weak smile. "I'm fine, Harriet, thanks again for the meal, I'll see you soon."

Vincent got a bit of work thanks to the card in the teashop door. The Misses Yardley asked him to come and change a lightbulb for them; he did it willingly and didn't want to charge them for it but they insisted. On Wednesday morning I had a surprise visit from Nell Unsworth. She'd popped in to look at the upstairs room and finalise arrangements for the next Saturday morning's art class but noticed the card on her way in. "I've been looking for an electrician," she said; "I could do with more plug sockets in my studio."

"I'll give him a ring and ask him to call in this afternoon to give you an estimate if you like."

"That's great. Ask him to leave it until after two thirty to make sure I'm in."

"I will. The knitting group is up in the room at the moment but I'm sure they won't mind if you nip up and take a look."

She was up and back down again in ten minutes. "The room's perfect for us," she said; "do you mind if we shift the furniture around a bit, we'll put it back before we leave."

"No problem," I said.

Vincent had only recently got home when I arrived and he was in the kitchen trying to decide what to cook for supper. "Hello Love," I called, "have you been to see Nell?"

He came into the living room. "Yes, in fact I've only just got back. What an interesting woman, I could have chatted to her all day."

"I don't know her that well," I said, kicking off my shoes and hunting for my slippers. "I've only met her a few times but I think she's someone I'd get on well with."

"Oh you definitely would. Er, she's invited me to join the Saturday morning art group."

"Really?" I abandoned my search, they must be in the bedroom. "I didn't know art was your thing."

He'd gone back into the kitchen so had to raise his voice for me to hear. "It hasn't been, in the past but I thought I'd give it a try; it's something to do."

I went into the kitchen and stood for a while on the cool vinyl tiles; my feet were on fire and it was so soothing. Eventually I said, "But you haven't got any equipment; surely you'll need some brushes and paints, if nothing else."

"Nell said the group will provide me with anything I need."

"That's good of them and if you take to it perhaps I could buy you some art stuff for Christmas."

"Perhaps," he said, "we'll see; I might not like it."

He was peeling potatoes at the sink. "What are we having?" I asked.

"Sausages and mash, if that's okay?"

My tummy rumbled in anticipation. "Wonderful," I said. "I think I'll go for a shower if you don't need me."

"Nope, I've got everything under control."

Chapter Eleven

The last place I wanted to be on a Friday evening after work was in the village hall at a fundraising meeting. The tearoom had been really busy all day and I was whacked. When I arrived at the hall I parked up next to another car and was surprised to see Nell, in the driving seat, smoking. When she saw me she stubbed out her cigarette in the ashtray on the dashboard and got out of the car. I smiled and said "Are you waiting until the last minute again?"

"No," she said with a laugh. "I was only waiting for someone else to arrive; Adele's in there on her own and I didn't want to have to make small talk with her."

"Don't you like her?"

"I've nothing against her, really but she somehow always manages to make me feel inferior."

I was shocked. "That really surprises me. I didn't think you were the type of person to let anyone intimidate you."

She gave a wry smile. "Even the hardest shells have a weak spot."

"Come on," I said, "let's go in; I'll look after you."

"By the way," said Nell, as we walked, "I'm impressed by that lad of yours; we had a great chat when he came to see me."

"I believe so."

"If I was twenty years younger and of a different persuasion I might be in danger of falling for him."

It took me a minute to understand what she meant by a 'different persuasion' but realised I was neither shocked or surprised. "That's a shame because he likes older women," I said with a chuckle. "His last partner was six years older than him."

"She was a fool to let go of him and she'll regret it, mark my words."

"I think it was more like pushing him away than letting him go," I said.

We walked into the hall together. The furniture was arranged as before but Adele was pacing up and down, looking at her watch. "Where is everyone?" she asked. "It's almost five to."

"No, your watch must be fast," said Nell "and I think I can hear voices outside."

As if on cue Dorothy and Belinda walked in together. "Is Wanda with you?" demanded Adele.

"She's just parking up," said Belinda, taking a seat at the table; Dorothy sat next to her and Nell and I sat opposite.

A few minutes later the door swung open and Wanda swept into the room with a large box under her arm. "Sorry I'm on the last minute," she said, breathlessly, "but I stopped to pick these up from the printers on my way here."

Nell jumped up and took the box from her; it looked quite heavy.

"Ah good," said Adele, starting to relax, "that will be the flyers; put them on the table please Nell, if you don't mind."

Nell obeyed and Adele took a pair of nail scissors from the handbag on her seat and promptly scored down the parcel tape sealing the lid. On top of the flyers lay the posters; she took one out and lifted it up for us all to see. "I hope that between us we can arrange to display them around the local villages," she said.

"I'll put one up in the tearoom," I said, "and I don't mind taking some of the flyers. It's my day off tomorrow and I'll deliver them around where I live."

The other ladies offered to take some as well and do the same in their areas. Wanda took her seat at the end of the table and produced her notepad. "I've already had some inquiries about stalls," she said, "and that's even before we put out the flyers so I've taken the names of those who have made a definite booking."

"Did you ask for a deposit?" asked Adele.

"No," said Wanda, "I didn't think it was necessary."

"They might change their minds at the last minute and let us down."

"Then we'd only have the inconvenience of returning their deposits."

"The deposits would be forfeit of course."

"Then I shall refer all enquiries to yourself, Adele," said Wanda shortly, "and you can be in charge of collecting deposits and returning them or not as you see fit." she snapped her notebook shut.

Adele opened her mouth to give a retort but obviously thought better of it when she saw the light of battle in Wanda's eyes. "Very well then, I will," she eventually said.

There followed a brief uncomfortable silence until Belinda spoke up. "Are there any more matters on the agenda, Adele?"

"Not unless *anyone else* has something," she said haughtily, glaring directly at Wanda.

"No," the rest of us piped up in unison.

"Then I suggest we meet again in two weeks for an update and any enquiries for stalls should be directed to myself."

"Well it is *your* telephone number on the posters and flyers," pronounced Wanda in an even tone.

"Precisely!" said Adele as she picked up her bag and flounced out of the hall, leaving the rest of us gaping after her.

"It's alright ladies," said Wanda, "you can take yourselves home; I'll lock up."

None of us needed telling twice. We all stood up and hastily took our leave.

"See you tomorrow, Harriet," said Nell when we reached the cars.

"No it's my day off tomorrow but Olive will look after you and see to anything you might need."

Chapter Twelve

As much as I loved having my son with me it was good to have a bit of time to myself when he went off to the art group. I smiled to myself as I washed the breakfast pots; perhaps my Vincent would become a famous artist like his namesake, Van Gogh - as long as he didn't decide to cut off his ear! I finished the washing up, made myself a coffee and settled myself in the armchair in the lounge with my book. I became absorbed in the plot and so was a little irritated when a knock at the door disturbed my peace. When I opened the door, however, I got a nice surprise; it was Dave.

"Oh Hello, Harriet, I didn't expect to see you," he said. " I thought you'd be working."

"Not today, it's my day off. Have you come to see Vincent?"

"Yes, is he in?"

"No, but come in anyway; have you time for a coffee?"

"Always," he said, following me into the living room and through to the kitchen."

"He's joined Nell Unsworth's art group," I said whilst I filled the kettle with water. "They've started using the upstairs room at the cafe on Saturday mornings."

"Is he into painting?"

"Not that I know of but he was quite taken with Nell when he went to see her about some work and she persuaded him to give it a try."

He hesitated before saying "I hope he's not smitten with her because…"

I stopped him by raising my hand. "I know but it's nothing like that, he simply found her good company."

When our drinks were ready we sat at the kitchen table. "Did you want Vincent for something in particular?" I asked.

"I wanted to drop off the directions for the job on Monday."

"You can leave them with me if you like and I'll pass them on."

He took a folded sheet of paper out of his pocket and put it on the table before asking "And what have you got planned for the rest of your day off?"

I sighed. "I'd like to say I'll be catching up with some housework but I'm struggling to work up the enthusiasm."

He smiled. "In that case, can I tempt you out for some lunch?"

I thought about it but not for long. "Give me a few minutes to make myself presentable."

"There's no rush but you look fine as you are."

I looked down at my faded blue joggers and sloppy Joe Tshirt. "Thanks for that," I said, "but I think I'll get changed anyway. Why don't you go through to the living room while you wait; you'll be more comfortable."

I looked in my wardroom and picked out some black leggings and a plain pale blue tunic top then I selected a long silver pendant and matching earrings to set the outfit off; a hint of eyeshadow and a touch of lipstick added the final touches. When I walked into the living room Dave gave me a wolf whistle. "Thank you kind sir," I said, "flattery will get you everywhere."

"That's what I'm hoping for," he said, with a cheeky grin.

"Behave yourself," I said, feeling a hot flush fill my cheeks but loving the banter.

Dave had parked his car behind mine on the road and as I climbed into the passenger seat my mobile phone rang. It was Vincent. "Hi Mum," he said, "I'm going to the pub for lunch with some of the art group, do you mind?"

"Not at all, I'm going out for lunch myself; I've left you a note on the kitchen table."

"Okay, I'll see you later then."

"Right," I said when I'd put my phone back in my bag, "where are you taking me?"

"I know a lovely little pub on the outskirts of Ambleside; I've not been for a while but I believe it's still got a fantastic reputation."

"Sounds good to me," I said.

It had been a long time since I'd had the luxury of being a passenger and I took full advantage of being able to admire the plush green rolling hills and the rich autumnal hues of orange, red and brown that adorned the trees lining the country lanes.

"You're quiet," said Dave, breaking into my reverie.

"Sorry, I'm just enjoying the scenery."

"And the company I hope," he said.

"Of course," I said with a smile.

The pub was wedged snuggly in between two shops in the centre of a small village not dissimilar to Underwood and from the outside was typical of any other lakeland building but when we walked through the front door I was pleasantly surprised by the modern decor but with enough of a hint of tradition not to look brash. Because of the time of year it was busy but not full to capacity so we easily found a table in the restaurant area. The menu was extensive for such a small establishment and it took us a while to choose but when the food was served it lived up to every expectation and as I wasn't driving I was able to indulge in a small glass of red.

When we'd finished eating we took our coffees into the bar where the seating was a little more comfortable. We settled ourselves at a table in the corner of the backrest where we were able to relax and let our meals digest. I opened the conversation by saying "I went to a fundraising meeting last night in the village hall and there was a bit of unpleasantness between Adele and Wanda Barraclough; do those two have history? It felt like it."

"I don't think so," he said, "apart from the fact that they are both strong minded women who like having their own way."

I thought about it. "Yes that's probably it."

"The thing is, with Adele," he continued, "since the children left home the village hall has become her baby and she's very protective of anything to do with it."

"I'm aware of that," I said, remembering how she challenged me about the upstairs room on our first meeting. "I didn't know she had children"

"Yes, two boys; they're both married now."

"Any grandchildren?"

He shook his head. "Not yet."

"But she sees her sons?"

"Oh yes, regularly but as you can imagine she doesn't make the best of mothers-in-law."

I could definitely imagine it but I kept my mouth shut and simply smiled.

"Speaking of sons," he said, "d'you think Vincent will be staying with you long term?"

I shrugged. "I honestly don't know and I don't think he does either."

"Would you like him to be?"

I didn't answer straight away but swirled the dregs of my coffee around my cup. "I want him to be happy," I said at last, "and I don't think he knows what to do for the best. I try not to interfere in the lives of my children but they know I'm there if they need me."

He stared at me for a moment. "Aren't you tempted, even a little, to give them advice?"

"No. If I have an opinion I keep it to myself, that way I can't be blamed if things go wrong."

"But what if you could see they were running headlong into disaster?"

"People have to be allowed to make their own mistakes, that's how they learn. All I can do is be there to help put back the pieces if they break."

"And how do you do that?"

"With love."

Dave stared down into his empty coffee cup and I was starting to think I'd said something wrong because the silence between us was becoming uncomfortable so pretending a need for the ladies, I excused myself. When I came back Dave seemed to have recovered himself and greeted me with a smile. "I'm ready for home now if you are," I said.

The drive home was just as pleasant as the outward journey with dusk beginning to fall and over to the west the setting sun was matching the trees for a magnificent display of colour. If I'd touched on a sensitive subject earlier there was no hint of it now and Dave seemed relaxed as we wound our way through the country lanes. When we arrived at my cottage he declined my invitation to come in for a coffee. "I need to be getting home." he said. "Tell Vincent I'll see him on Monday."

"I will," I said, climbing out of the car.

I waved him off and watched him drive away before going inside. Vincent was already home. "Had a nice time?" he asked.

"Yes, lovely, thanks. Did you?"

"Yes, great," he said.

I looked around the living room. "Well, come on, where is it? Let's see the masterpiece."

"What?"

"The painting you did this morning, where is it?"

"Oh it was rubbish so I ripped it up and threw it in the bin."

"That's a shame but did you enjoy it?"

"Yes it was good, anyway, what's the score with you and Dave?"

"There is no score, we're just friends."

"Have you known him for long?"

"Only a few weeks actually," I said, putting my handbag by the armchair and sitting down. "He comes to the book club that's started meeting at the cafe."

"I see. Does he live on his own?"

I had to smile at his delicate probing. "I believe so, it seems he's been divorced for some years."

"Did *he* tell you that?"

"No, Olive did. Why?"

"I'm only looking out for you like any good son would."

He came and sat on the arm of the chair and hugged me. I patted his hand. "I know you are but there's no need to worry about me."

Chapter Thirteen

Vincent started his new job on the following Monday morning and seemed much happier now he had the prospect of earning a regular income again. I said as much to Dave when he came to the book club the next day. "He's settled in really well," he said. "The other men took to him straight away; they can tell he's a grafter."

That made me feel good because you still worry about your children's welfare no matter how grown up they are. We were interrupted at that point by the arrival of Dorothy Green. "I can see you've put the poster up in the door," she said, "have you delivered any flyers yet?"

"My two part-timers, Bradley and Sophie, have taken some to deliver near where they live and I'm going to take some round near me when I get home tonight."

"I could take some out for you," said Dave.

"I'm surprised Adele hasn't already roped you in," said Dorothy.

"Oh she has. I've already delivered some for *her*." he said with a chuckle.

They went upstairs together and I didn't see them at break time as I was busy in the kitchen and by the time I'd finished they'd all gone home. I was disappointed that Dave hadn't stayed for a drink but Olive cut into my thoughts. "Dave said to say goodbye; he had to dash off but he's taken a stack of flyers to deliver."

I was a little mollified but I couldn't get over the niggle of suspicion that I'd upset him in   some way when we'd had lunch together.

The next morning when Kathleen Thomas came for the knitting group, I asked her "Is your group having a stall at the table top sale?"

"Yes, I've contacted Adele but I haven't had time to take the deposit yet."

Carrie, the post girl, had come in behind her and overheard our conversation. "I can take it for you, if you like," she said, "I'm calling there later to pay ours."

"Would you, love? That's kind of you," said Kathleen, taking a five pound note out of her purse. "Are you having a stall then?"

"Gran and I are having one between us; she makes cuddly toys and I make jewellery."

"I didn't know that," I said. "How long have you been doing it?"

"Gran's sewn for years but I only started making the jewellery a few months ago after I did a course at the shop in Illingsby. I haven't got a lot of stock yet; that's why Gran's sharing the stall with me."

"I'll look forward to seeing your work," I said. "Have you time for a cuppa?"

She looked at her watch. "Yes, why not. Have you heard from Rose lately?"

Before I could answer, the front door opened and my son, Vincent came stalking in.

"Hello," I said, "Are you not working today?"

"I have been but my part of the job is finished for the moment while we wait for some materials so I thought I'd come and have breakfast."

Carrie was looking on with interest. "You haven't met my son, have you? Carrie, this is Vincent and Vincent, this is Carrie, our postgirl and a good friend of mine."

"Pleased to meet you Carrie," said Vincent, holding out his hand.

"Likewise," said Carrie, taking it to shake.

"Why don't the two of you take a seat and bring you both over some breakfast."

The rest of the knitters were starting to arrive so both Olive and I were kept busy for a while. When I had a chance, I looked up and saw Vincent sitting on his own, finishing his coffee. I went over to him. "Has Carrie gone?"

"Yes, she said thank you for her breakfast but she had to get back to her deliveries. She would have thanked you herself but you were busy."

"I'm sorry I missed her, it's ages since we've had time for a real chat."

"Well as a matter of fact she invited me to the quiz night at the pub tonight, why don't you come as well?"

"But if the invitation was for you?"

"No, it wasn't like that; she said their team was short of members so you'd probably be more than welcome."

"In that case I think it's a great idea."

The pub was getting quite full by the time we arrived but Carrie had saved us some seats and was looking out for us. "I'm glad you could make it, Harriet, when I mentioned it to Vincent he said he would try and get you to come as well."

"Who else is on the team?" I asked.

"Tonight there's only me and Dad; he's at the bar. My brother sometimes comes but he can't make it this evening."

Vincent got up to go to the bar to get us some drinks and as I watched him make his way through the tables I spotted a familiar face. Dave Kenyon was sitting in the corner with Fred Thomas and another man who was so like Dave that it had to be his brother. I asked Carrie if I was right.

"Yes, that's Brian Kenyon, Adele's husband. He was at home when I called with the deposits."

Dave hadn't seen me and at that point Carrie's dad came back from the bar with Vincent in tow. "Hello, Harriet," he said. "Carrie said she was hoping you and your son would join us, we need all the help we can get."

"You speak for yourself, cheeky," said Carrie, taking the half pint of lager he offered her and they both laughed.

Once the quiz started we gave it our full attention and it was obvious that Alan Gordon had been being modest beforehand. We didn't win but we gave a good account of ourselves and I really enjoyed it. I felt like my brain had been given a workout. "Please say you'll come again next week, Harriet, we've been trying to get Mum to come and she might do so if she knows you'll be here."

I'd only met Millie Gordon a few times but I liked her and thought I would enjoy her company so I said "Okay."

"What about you, Vincent? You can't leave me to be outnumbered by the females."

"I wouldn't dream of letting that happen," said Vincent with mock severity.

I stood up to put my coat on and spotted Dave standing by the bar; he'd seen me. He smiled and waved and I did the same before I was ushered out of my seat and towards the front door. "Come on Mum," said Vincent. "We've both got an early start in the morning."

"Are you going to the art group tomorrow?" I asked Vincent before I went to bed on Friday night.

"No, I'm going over to Nell's first thing though; I'm going to put those sockets in for her while she's out."

"I expect that's the best time for her so you don't interrupt her work."

"That's what she said."

"I might see you in the morning before I leave. Will you be in for dinner?"

"Yes, I should be finished by then."

"I'll bring something home with me then we don't have to cook."

I was glad I'd decided to do that because we had a particularly busy day and the last thing I felt like doing when I got home was to start cooking something completely from scratch. Vinvent was in his bedroom so I knocked quietly on the door.

"Come in ,Mum," he called.

When I opened the door he was sitting on the bed and I could tell by his expression that something was wrong. If I didn't know my son like I did I'd have thought he'd been crying. I sat next to him. "What's the matter?" I asked.

"Don't go mad at me but I phoned Elaine."

It wasn't what I wanted to hear but I tried not to let it show. "I won't go mad but I can tell it didn't go well."

"I rang to ask her if I could drive over tomorrow to see the boys and perhaps take them out but she said they were staying with their *real* dad for the weekend."

"She didn't actually say that, did she?"

"Oh yes, she did."

I could feel the anger bubbling up inside me and in my head I called her the nastiest name I could think of but would never say out loud. I put my arm around his shoulder as he continued. "I know I'm not their biological father but I feel like they are my own and I know they feel the same about me."

There was nothing I could say or do to ease his pain so I settled for a hug. When he broke away from the embrace he looked at me and said "This might sound awful, Mum, but I've realised I miss the boys so much but I don't miss Elaine at all."

"It doesn't sound awful at all," I said. "It's completely understandable."

The next day was Sunday and my day off but before I knew it Monday morning was here and I was back behind the counter. Although he hadn't mentioned it again I knew

Vincent was still upset about not seeing the boys. Luckily, I had Olive to confide in and was able to get everything I felt about Elaine, off my chest. Never one to mince her words Olive gave vent to her own feelings on the matter. "In my opinion he's better off without her; she didn't know when she had a good 'un."

"I totally agree," I said and told her what he'd said about missing the boys but not Elaine.

"It would be the best thing for him if he could find a nice girl and settle down near here." she said.

I didn't want to speak it out loud but the same thought had crossed *my* mind. "You never know," I said, "when he's had time to put his heart back together."

Our conversation was interrupted by the arrival of Wanda Barraclough with a notepad under her arm. "Good morning ladies," she said with a wide smile.

"Good morning," replied Olive and I in unison. "What can we get you?" I asked.

"An americano with cold milk and no sugar please and I've also come begging."

"I'll get the coffee," said Olive, "and you deal with the other matter, Harriet."

Wanda took a seat at an empty table by the counter and I joined her. "How can I help?" I asked.

"I don't have a stall to run at the sale," she said, "so I thought I'd organise a raffle."

"Good idea," I said. "Would you like me to donate a prize?"

She grinned. "That would be lovely, if you don't mind."

"How about a voucher for afternoon tea for two?" I offered.

"Perfect!" she said, "I knew I could rely on you."

"Have you asked anyone else yet?"

"Oh yes, Nell is donating a couple of coffee mugs and the Jamieson's are putting together a grocery hamper."

"Why don't you ask Clara Phillips? She might donate something from the gift shop."

"She's next on my list."

She put her notebook down on the table while she wrote down my donation and I glanced at the others on the list and spotted a familiar name. "I see you've got Dave Kenyon down for something."

"Yes he's offered two hours of his time as a handyman."

Seeing his name brought another thought into my head. "Does…? I mean have you…?"

She started to chuckle. "Yes, I have run this by Adele and she has sanctioned it."

I had to smile. "Sorry but…"

She stopped me. "No need to apologise; no-one knows better than me how fragile our lady chairwoman's ego is so I wouldn't dream of acting without her say so."

"You mean like promising people, table hire without a deposit," I said cheekily.

She laughed. "Don't get me started on that one. Let's say I've learned my place."

Olive came over with the coffee.

"I expect you'll be helping Harriet with the refreshments at the table top sale," said Wanda.

"I don't know," she said with a haughty look down her nose at me. "I haven't been asked yet."

"Sorry," I said, looking up at her "but when did you ever need to be asked to join the party?"

She seemed to consider this and then shrugged. "Point taken," she said.

Chapter Fourteen

Dave was first to arrive for the book club and he greeted me with a smile. "I hear you're offering your services as a raffle prize," I said.

He nodded. "Dorothy is organising a second hand book stall on behalf of the group and I wanted to do my bit so it was either a barrowful of bricks or me."

I pretended to mull this over. "Mm it's difficult to know which of them people would prefer."

He pointed his book at me. "Don't be cheeky, you."

"As if." I said innocently but then spoiled it by laughing.

"Actually, Harriet, I was wondering if you'd have time for a coffee and a chat after the meeting."

"I should think so, we're not usually very busy at that time."

"Great," he said. "Ah here's Kevin, he can help me set the chairs up."

Olive had been clearing tables and came back to the counter as the men were going upstairs. She nodded her head in their direction. "How are things progressing between you and him?"

"Who Kevin? I hardly know the man."

She gave me one of her looks.

"I've told you there is no me and him; he's simply a customer who's become a friend."

"Alright," she said with a sigh as she made her way into the kitchen with the dirty pots, "I'll ask no more but give me plenty of time to buy a hat before the wedding."

"It's a good job you're carrying that tray," I called after her but all I heard in reply was a giggle.

The rest of the book club members had left when Dave came down the stairs as he'd volunteered to collect the last of the crockery they'd used. By the time he placed the laden tray on the counter the cafe was empty and Olive had gone home. I put the snip on the lock and the closed sign on the door. "Shall I take this tray into the kitchen for you?" he asked.

"If you don't mind. In fact if you could put the dirty pots in the dishwasher for me while I make the coffees they can be washed while we're having our drinks."

"I see. Making use of my services already and you haven't even won me in the raffle yet."

"Not at all," I said indignantly, "I'm going to pay you - in coffee and cake of course."

"It's a deal," he said, disappearing into the kitchen.

I placed the drinks and cakes on one of the tables and waited for Dave to join me. "What you're short of in here," he said, "is a couple of tables with sofas, like those in the room upstairs."

"Well we could take our drinks upstairs if you prefer."

He grinned. "It's been a long time since I got a proposition like that, Harriet, you saucy thing."

I felt my cheeks go red hot and searched for a suitable retort but he put me out of my misery.

"Sorry, I didn't mean to embarrass you; I was only teasing."

I knew he had been and started to laugh. "And it's been a long time since a bloke made me blush like that."

He decided to change the subject. "I didn't realise you were a quizzer."

"A quizzer? Oh you mean at the pub last week. Carrie had been in that morning and invited Vincent and I to join their team. She made us promise to go again this week. We really enjoyed it so it might become a regular thing."

"That's a shame, I was hoping to poach you onto our team; we could do with some female knowledge."

"Well you're too late, I'm afraid. Hang on, is that why you wanted to meet me for a coffee?"

His face became serious as he pulled his piece of cake towards him. "No, actually, I wanted to talk about when we went out for lunch."

"Oh, I see. Why?"

"You must have noticed that I went quiet just before we left."

"Yes, I did," I admitted. "I thought I might have offended you in some way."

He shook his head. "It was when you were talking about your family and how close you are; it touched a nerve."

"I'm sorry, I didn't realise."

"It's not *your* fault, you weren't to know but I have a son whom I haven't seen since he was a child. His mother and I got divorced years ago and she refused to let me have contact with him."

"But she couldn't do that. You had a right to see him."

He looked me in the eye and I could tell he was struggling. "It was my fault, you see, I had an affair and when she found out she left me, taking George with her. In the divorce settlement I gave her everything she asked for but she took from me the only thing I wanted; to keep in touch with my son."

"You must have been granted contact."

"Yes, I was but once the divorce went through she moved out of the area and didn't leave a forwarding address. I tried everything I could to track them down but it was as if they'd disappeared off the face of the earth."

I couldn't help comparing it to Vincent's situation and thinking how much more it must hurt if they were your own flesh and blood.

"I'm not proud of what I did, Harriet but I've paid for every moment of that affair."

"It's brave of you to tell me." I said.

"You must think badly of me now."

"No, we all make mistakes and have regrets."

"It's kind of you to say so but I bet you never betrayed your husband."

No I hadn't; he was the love of my life and I'd never been tempted to stray. What's the saying 'Why dine out on beefburger when you have steak at home. "I was lucky," I said, "I met my one and only, first time, that doesn't happen to everyone."

"You must miss him."

"I do, sometimes more than others but life goes on and he wouldn't want me to grieve forever."

I took hold of his hand which was resting on the table by the untouched piece of cake. "Come on, let's drink our coffees before they get cold and I'll be insulted if you don't eat that cake."

He put his other hand over mine and said. "I like you, Harriet Jones."

"I like you too, Dave Kenyon."

Chapter Fifteen

Vincent and I attended the quiz night as promised and I was pleased to see that Carrie had persuaded her mother to join us and to complete the team, her brother, Terry, as well. As I took my seat I glanced round the room and spotted Fred Thomas sitting on his own but before I had time to realise how disappointed I was the door opened and in walked Dave with his brother. Brian made straight for Fred's table but Dave stopped and looked round; when he spotted me he smiled and weaved his way through the tables to ours.

"I think this is grossly unfair," he said with mock severity; "you have an abundance of female knowledge on this team while ours is sadly lacking."

"Hard cheese," said Alan Gordon. "I hope you weren't thinking of trying to steal someone."

Dave laughed and held up his hands. "I come in peace," he said, "but I would like to borrow Harriet for a few minutes to introduce her to my brother."

I ignored the raised eyebrows around me as I stood to go with him. "You'd better let her come back," said Alan, "or we'll send someone over to rescue her."

"I promise, scout's honour," he said, making a salute.

"I didn't know you'd been in the scouts," I said as I followed him through the tables.

"Well I was. To be honest there's not much else to occupy a young boy around here and it kept me out of trouble."

"Pity you're not still a member then," I said innocently behind his back.

He stopped and turned and I saw the twinkle in his eye. "That's why I need a friend like you."

Brian and Fred were deep in conversation when we approached their table but they stopped and looked up when they realised we were there. "Brian, this is Harriet Jones, a friend of mine and one of Adele's latest recruits."

Brian stood and shook my hand. "Pleased to meet you, Harriet. My wife thinks highly of you which puts you in a very exclusive club."

"Are you joining our team, Harriet?" asked Fred hopefully. "We could do with some female knowledge."

"Sorry Fred I'm spoken for but why don't you bring Kathleen?"

He gave me a withering look. "You must be joking. She says she encourages me to come so she can have a bit of peace."

"What about Adele?" I said to Brian.

All three men looked at me in horror as if I'd suggested that Attilla the Hun join their team but it was Brian who spoke. "I love my wife very much but let's say it's the time apart that helps us to appreciate each other when we're together."

Dave patted him on the back and laughed. "Well said brother."

People were starting to go up for their quiz sheets so I said "It's nice to meet you Brian but I think my team needs me."

When I got back to the table, Alan had gone for the quiz sheets and Vincent and Terry were at the bar so I was leapt on by my other teammates. Carrie was never one to let a good question go unasked. "Is there something we should know about you and Dave Kenyon?"

"Only that we've become friends through his coming to the book club at the cafe."

She squinted her eyes. "Friends?"

"Yes," I said, "*Friends*. We get on really well."

"Vincent said he took you out to lunch."

"Did he now?"

Carrie and Millie continued to look at me with smiles playing around their lips.

"Alright, I admit I enjoy his company and he seems to enjoy mine but we're not what you young people call an 'item' by any means."

That seemed to satisfy them and soon the men were back and the quiz started.

The next Saturday was my day off; Vincent had decided to give the art group another go so I was looking forward to some time to myself and getting round to some jobs I'd been putting off for ages. I started by allowing myself a leisurely breakfast of doorstep toast, topped liberally with butter and marmalade and then set about emptying one of the kitchen cupboards so that I could wipe down the inside. When the knocker banged on the door I was, at first, a little irritated at the interruption but then a spark of excitement rumbled round my tummy at the thought that it might be Dave wanting to go out for lunch again. The broad smile that lit up my face turned upside down when I opened the door.

"Hello Harriet, is Vincent in?"

"I'm afraid not, Elaine, was he expecting you?"

"No, I thought I'd surprise him. Will he be back soon?"

"You'd better come in," I said, reluctantly opening the door wide to let her pass. "Are the boys not with you?"

"No, they're with Mum. I thought Vincent and I could do with some time alone to talk things through."

I felt my heart sink to my boots; she'd probably heard that he was earning again and wanted her meal ticket back. I painted on my best attempt at a smile and went to put the kettle on while she made herself comfortable in the armchair. When I came back with two mugs of coffee she was putting her phone back in her bag. "I've tried to ring him but there's no answer so I've left him a message, letting him know I'm here."

I wasn't going to tell her where he was so I said "I expect he'll get back to you as soon as he can." I hoped he got the message sooner rather than later because the last thing I felt like doing was spending my day off with this woman. He must have looked at his phone as soon as the art class finished and come straight home because he arrived shortly before twelve thirty. I could tell by the look on his face when he came through the door that his guest wasn't exactly welcome. He made an exaggerated sweep of the room with his eyes. "Where are the boys, didn't you bring them with you?"

"They've been invited to a birthday party."

"I thought you said they were with your mum," I put in.

"Yes they are," she said with only a moment's hesitation. "She's taking them to the party for me."

"So why are you here?" asked Vincent, getting straight to the point.

She glanced in my direction. "Like I said to your mum, there are things we need to talk about."

I thought of making myself scarce but then decided against it; why should I? This was my home. I settled myself into the other armchair making it obvious I was there to stay.

"What do you need to say to me that couldn't be discussed over the phone?" asked Vincent.

"Well, I suppose I wanted to see you as well," replied Elaine, looking sheepishly up at him. "I thought we might go out for lunch."

Vincent gave a wry smile. We all knew who would be footing the bill.

"I could rustle up something here," I said innocently and could have laughed out loud at the look she gave me.

"No, you're alright Mum, I don't want to put you to any trouble. There's a greasy spoon on the road to Inglesby and if we go in separate cars Elaine can be off home as soon as we've eaten. I think that'll give us enough time to say what needs to be said."

Elaine's lips pursed together as if she had just sucked on a lemon but then she recovered herself. "That sounds perfect."

When they'd gone I made myself a sandwich but when I sat down to eat it, it felt like sawdust in my mouth and the churning in my stomach was making me feel nauseous. Vincent might have put on a good show of indifference while I was there but I knew from past experience how well she could manipulate him when she turned on the charm. In the end I gave up trying to eat and went back to what I was doing before Elaine interrupted me; it would help take my mind off what was happening with my son. It had almost succeeded when I heard him come through the front door and throw his van keys on the coffee table. We met in the kitchen doorway.

"She's gone then?"

"Oh yes," he said. "She got what she came for and left."

"Which was?"

"The usual, money of course. She said the boys wanted to go on a school trip and she couldn't afford it."

"But you've been sending money for the boys, I know you have, even though they're not really your responsibility."

"I know but she gave me the sob story about how much growing boys cost to bring up and how much they would be disappointed if they couldn't go because they'd be the only ones in the class."

"And you fell for it."

"Of course. She knows which buttons to press."

"But she wasn't prepared to bring them to see you."

He sat down heavily on the settee and put his head in his hands. At first I thought he was crying but when he looked up at me he was dry eyed.

"She said I could go and collect them and bring them here for a couple of days during the Christmas holidays."

I wasn't taken in. "So you'd be an unpaid babysitter while she went to work."

He nodded, resignedly. "I know you're right but at least I'll get to spend some time with them; at this rate by the time I get to see them I'll be like a stranger."

I sat down next to him and put my arm around his shoulders. "She knows exactly how you feel about those boys and I'm afraid she will always use that knowledge to her advantage."

He looked me straight in the eye. "I'd like to think those boys will always be in my life but I really wouldn't care if I never set eyes on their mother again."

I could have said 'That makes two of us' but I restrained myself. "I hope by giving her the money you didn't leave yourself short of cash."

For the first time in our conversation he smiled. "Oh I didn't hand over any cash; I told her I'd do a bank transfer to the school."

I couldn't stop myself from laughing out loud. "I don't think she'll be visiting us again in a hurry."

"I wouldn't bank on it, Mum. It's hard to dislodge leeches when they get their teeth into you."

Chapter Sixteen

The Lake District National Park is considered by some to be at its loveliest during the Autumn months, providing a magnificent spectacle of colour before the trees shed their leaves for Winter. This means a welcome boom in the tourist trade and a very busy time for the area's businesses before they too wind down for the quiet season after Christmas.

Clara Philips decided she would close the gift shop after the New Year holiday which was perfect for the village hall fundraising committee. Stalls were selling fast for the table top sale which promised that there would be enough money for at least the first couple of month's rent of the shop.

It had been two weeks since Elaine's visit and Vincent hadn't heard a peep from her, not that he seemed bothered. He was getting enough work to give him a decent income and he seemed content with his life in the country. Although he insisted that none of his efforts were good enough to show me, his interest in the art group hadn't waned and I thought I'd ask Nell to give me some idea of what I might buy him for Christmas; he couldn't carry on borrowing from the other members of the group, it wasn't fair.

Left on my own again on my Saturday off I decided to do some batch baking for the tea room but when I looked in the cupboard I realised I was short of flour and sugar. It wasn't too big a problem' I knew we had plenty in the storeroom over the tearoom and decided to nip down and pick some up.

Olive was in the kitchen when I let myself in through the back door; she was buttering bread for sandwiches and looked up when I came in. "Hello Harriet, have you forgotten it's your day off?"

"No of course not," I said as I peeped into the cafe. Most of the tables were occupied but Brad and Sophie had everything under control. "I've come to pick up some flour and sugar from the storeroom upstairs."

Olive put out a hand to stop me heading for the stairs. "I'll ask Brad to go up and get it for you; save you carrying it down the stairs."

"What are you implying?" I said with a laugh, "that I'm too old and infirm to carry a couple of bags of flour and sugar down a flight of stairs."

"No, of course not but why not let a pair of young legs take the strain."

"Brad and Sophie are both busy and besides I thought I'd have a sneak peek into the art class to see how Vincent is getting on. He won't show me any of his paintings."

Before she could stop me I was on the stairs. As I reached the top I could hear Nell's voice giving advice to the group so as silently as I could, I opened the door a sliver and looked round the group to look for Vincent. I could see half a dozen artists standing in front of easels but he wasn't one of them so I opened the door a little wider. A couple more artists came into my view and also Nell who was pointing out something about the model's pose. The model was reclining on one of the couches with his back to me but then Nell asked him to change position and he turned to face me.

I was about to quickly shut the door so as not to seem like I was a peeping Tom but then I opened it wide as recognition dawned on me. "Vincent!"

"Mum!"

Suddenly every pair of eyes in the room was on me as I took in the sight of my son in all his glory. An uncomfortable silence filled the room until I ripped it apart by bursting out laughing. Vincent had hastily covered his modesty with a length of fabric which had previously adorned the couch he'd been lying on and the look on his face made me laugh even louder. "I'm sorry," I said, wiping the tears from my eyes with the back of my hand, "but it was such a shock."

"But you don't mind?" asked Vincent.

"Why on earth should I mind," I said, calming down at last. "If you've got it, flaunt it, as they say."

I explained briefly why I was there and then left them to continue. I was still giggling when I reached Olive who was waiting for me in the kitchen. She looked like she was expecting to be told off. "You knew, didn't you?" I asked.

"Yes but I was sworn to secrecy."

"I see now why you wanted to send Brad upstairs for the flour and sugar. It was nothing to do with saving my legs."

"No, it was more to do with saving Vincent's embarrassment."

"I don't know why he should be embarrassed, it's not the first time I've seen his bits and pieces."

"No," she said with a laugh, "but it's probably the first time you've witnessed him displaying them in public."

I was washing up the last of my pots and pans when Vincent arrived home; he came straight through to the kitchen to join me. "Oh hello," I said, "it's my son, the male model."

We both started to laugh. "You didn't half give me a shock when I saw you standing in the doorway," he said.

"Not half as big a shock as I got but at least now I know why you only went to the art group when it was my day off; I was beginning to think you were avoiding me."

"I'm sorry I didn't tell you," he said as he picked up a tea towel to help me dry the dishes, "but I didn't know how you'd feel about me doing it and it was an easy way of making a bit of cash while I was looking for work."

I stopped mid-scour and looked up at him, smiling. "Well son, you've got a good body and if people are willing to pay you to let them draw it then good luck to you."

"So you weren't embarrassed?"

"No, Vincent, I'm proud of you; although it's snookered what I was going to buy you for Christmas. I'll have to think of something else now."

"Just one thing though Mum."

"What's that?""Please don't tell Naiomi."

"Spoilsport!" I said as I flicked soap suds into his face.

Chapter Seventeen

Olive arrived bright and early for work on Monday morning but didn't greet me with her usual smile. "Have you heard the news?" she blurted out almost before she came through the door.

"No," I said. "What's happened?"

"There's been a fire in the village hall."

I almost dropped the tray of clean cups I was carrying. "Oh no, has there been much damage?"

"The building itself is still standing but I believe the inside is a complete mess. I met P.C. Richards on my way here and he told me about it."

"Adele will be devastated," I said. "Do they know how it started?"

"Not yet, I think they are still investigating it."

"I expect this means that the table top sale might have to be cancelled."

"That's such a shame," said Olive. "So many people will be disappointed if it is."

Not long afterwards the members of the creative writing group started to arrive and they were all talking about the fire. There was much speculation but no-one knew any real facts so we were still none the wiser. It was the middle of the afternoon before we were visited by someone in the know. Adele and Wanda were arguing as they came through the door; in fact we heard their raised voices before they were even in sight. I gave Olive a knowing look and left my place behind the counter to greet them.

"Good afternoon ladies," I said, ushering them towards a table in a quiet corner of the room. "We've heard the news; what's the latest?"

Wanda opened her mouth to speak but Adele was in there first. "It's a complete nightmare. Thankfully no damage has been done to the structure of the building but the inside is ruined."

She plonked herself down at the table and covered her face with her hands. Wanda gave her a withering look but took the opportunity to speak. "We had a birthday party booked into the hall late Sunday afternoon and it's thought that someone sneaked a sly cigarette and threw the stub into a bin without making sure it was completely extinguished and the bin was full of wrapping paper."

Adele's head snapped up. "I've told you time and again how important it is to stress our no smoking rule when you take a booking."

"I always do but there was no-one there to make sure people keep to it. Didn't Brian notice anything untoward when he went to lock up?"

Adele's face flushed bright red. "Brian didn't lock up. I was out visiting a friend and called on my way home to do it."

Wanda's lips formed into a grimace but before she could speak, I interrupted. "Who reported the fire?"

"A local resident," said Wanda, "who was out walking his dog."

"That was lucky or it could have been a lot worse."

"Lucky!" exclaimed Adele. "You haven't seen the state of it; the table top sale will have to be cancelled for sure."

"But if it's only the interior that's damaged," I said, "surely we can do something about it."

"We've only got two weeks," stressed Adele.

"A lot can be achieved in two weeks if we put our minds to it."

Before Adele could protest further Wanda asked "What did you have in mind, Harriet?"

"I think the first job is for someone or a group of people to make a list of all the jobs that need doing and prioritise them in order of urgency."

"I could ask Brian and his brother Dave to do that," said Adele, becoming a little calmer now an action plan was being formed. "They'll know what to look for."

"Good idea," I said, "then call a meeting of the hall committee to organise a workforce."

Adele had thought of another problem. "Where's the money going to come from to pay for all the work?"

"Surely we have enough tradesmen and interested people in our community who would give their services for free," I suggested.

"That's a brilliant idea," said Wanda "but I've just thought of something. With the hall not fit to be used we've nowhere to hold a committee meeting."

"You could use my upstairs room," I said. "It's free on Wednesday afternoon if you can contact everyone by then."

I did realise that this offer might be a bit insensitive considering previous events and I could tell by the look on Adele's face that the irony wasn't lost on her but before she could protest Wanda spoke. "Thanks, Harriet, that would be perfect. I'll make a start on contacting members of the committee as soon as I get home."

"And I'll get Brian and Dave to do their bit as soon as they can," put in Adele, who seemed to have come to terms with the situation. "Will you be able to attend the meeting, Harriet?"

"I'll already be here but I'll be working; if we're not too busy I'll see if Olive can hold the fort while I join you, even if it's only for a few minutes."

I offered to make the ladies a drink but they both decided to get off home to begin the jobs they'd taken on. I knew Adele had done her bit when I got home that evening because Vincent said that Dave had asked him to go to the hall and check the electrics. "I'm meeting him and Brian first thing in the morning," he said.

When Dave arrived for the book club I asked him for an update and he was optimistic. "It looks as though the damage is mostly cosmetic and confined to the main room where the fire started. We've been lucky because if the fire hadn't been noticed so early it could have been a lot worse."

"I said that to Adele and she jumped down my throat."

"She's worried that's all."

"I know. Still, there'll be a lot of work to be done to get it ready for the table top sale."

"I've already been roped in," said Dave with a wry grin. "This semi-retirement is hard work; I never have a minute."

"You know you love it," I said, "you'd only get bored if you'd nothing to do."

"Chance'd be a fine thing," he muttered under his breath as he headed for the stairs.

It was becoming a regular thing that he would stay on, after the club, for a coffee and a chat and today was no exception but when he came down the stairs I had the feeling that he had something on his mind."

"Is something wrong?" I asked placing the two cups of coffee between us on the table.

He looked surprised. "No, what makes you ask?"

"You seem a little distracted as if there's something bothering you."

He smiled and looked me in the eye. "I didn't realise I was so transparent," he said; "or do you have a super power that allows you to read a person's thoughts?"

I laughed. "Now that would be telling but seriously I suppose I am really sensitive to people's moods; whether or not you'd call that a super power, I don't know."

He stirred his latte with the long spoon from the side of his saucer before he spoke. "You're right, I do have something on my mind and you might think it's foolish but I've hired a private detective."

I wasn't expecting that. "Really? What for?"

He looked up. "To help me find my son."

For once in my life I was lost for words so he continued. "After our conversation, the other day, I've not been able to stop thinking about George so I decided to do something about it. When they first left I tried everything I could to find them but found no trace so I thought I'd put it in the hands of a professional."

"Where did you find the private detective?" I asked. "I wouldn't know where to start."

"Online." He smiled. "What a wonderful tool the internet is, whatever did we do without it? Anyway there was quite a list; more than you would imagine but this guy specialises in tracking down missing people."

"Is it expensive?" I'd never known anyone who'd hired a private detective before; to me they were the subjects of films and television dramas.

"It's not cheap but if he manages to put me in touch with George it'll be worth every penny.

I reached across the table and took his hand. "I really hope he does, for George's sake as much as yours."

"Thanks, Harriet, but even if he does find him he may not want to see me after how I treated his mother."

I understood what he meant; Dave was the first person to admit he'd behaved badly towards his wife and she had returned the hurt in the way she'd known would cause the most pain. It was human nature to retaliate in this way and who knew what bitterness she'd passed on to their son. Dave could be in for intense joy or desperate heartache. I squeezed his hand. "There's not much I can do to help," I said, "but I'm always happy to listen and give what support I can."

He took my hand in both of his. "Thank you, that means a lot to me."

Chapter Eighteen

The lunchtime rush was finally ebbing when members of the fundraising committee began to arrive. Adele was first, as usual, but Dorothy was hot on her heels. "Good afternoon ladies," I said from behind the counter, "can I get you some drinks?"

"I'll have an americano please," stated Adele, "decaff, warm milk and no sugar."

"And I'll have a latte please," said Dorothy, smiling behind Adele's back.

"Okay, if you would like to show Adele up to the room, Dorothy, I'll be up in a minute with your drinks."

They couldn't have reached the top of the stairs when Wanda walked through the door clutching a plastic envelope folder. "Nell's parking the car," she said as she made her way towards me. "Mine's in the garage for a service so she gave me a lift and Belinda sends her apologies; one of the children is off school with a tummy bug."

"Oh that's a shame," I said. "Dorothy and Adele are already upstairs and I'm just making drinks; what would you like?"

"Coffee please, anyway it comes but no sugar. Do you need me to carry some cups for you?"

"No thanks, you're fine, I'll ask Nell to help me when she arrives."

A few minutes later Nell came breezing in through the door with a broad grin on her face. "Good afternoon, Harriet, good afternoon, Olive," she said. "How are things with you two?"

"Fine," we said in stereo.

"Good," she said. "I thought you might be cross with me, Harriet, for persuading your son to bare all in the name of art."

"I laughed. "He's old enough to make those decisions for himself and in fact I'd like to thank you for giving the opportunity to make a bit of cash when he needed it."

"No problem. I can see you're making drinks; do you need some help taking them upstairs?"

"Yes please," I said and before I could ask her what she wanted to drink, Olive placed a large cappuccino on the tray. It had extra chocolate sprinkles and a gingerbread biscuit on the side.

"Olive, you know me so well," exclaimed Nell with a chuckle.

"Well some people are so predictable," said Olive, turning away to hide a smile.

Still chuckling, Nell picked up the laden tray and headed for the stairs.

"Can you manage without me for a little while?" I asked Olive.

"Yes, I can give you a shout if I need you."

I reached the top of the stairs as Nell was distributing the drinks and I could hear Adele's voice.

"How come you've got a biscuit," she said, sounding piqued.

"Because I'm Olive's favourite," said Nell, with a straight face.

"It's okay ladies," I said, entering the room and placing a plateful on the table. "I've brought enough for everyone."

Adele seemed mollified by that and we all took a seat in the comfy chairs. Adele then opened the meeting and asked Wanda to read out the list of jobs that needed doing.

"First of all," said Wanda, "although the hall is in a bad state, it is mainly cosmetic. Dave Kenyon and Vincent Jones have assured us that the structure of the building is sound and the electrics have not been damaged."

"That's a relief," said Dorothy. We all nodded in unison.

"However," continued Wanda, "it still leaves us with a lot of work to do if we're to be ready for the table top sale."

"With that in mind," interrupted Adele, "I am in the process of putting together a posse of volunteers and the first job is to clean away all of the smoke damage before we can repaint."

"On that note," began Wanda with a piercing look at Adele, "Fred Thomas has offered to get us what we need at cost price and will lead the redecoration team. He says we can pay him for the paint when the insurance comes through."

"It would appear that you two ladies have got everything in hand," said Nell. "When do we start?"

"As soon as possible," said Adele. "My cleaning team will meet at the hall at nine o' clock tomorrow morning; I've asked everyone to bring their own mops and buckets etc. but we have some detergent in the cleaning cupboard."

"I can give a couple of hours," said Nell.

"So can I," said Dorothy.

I felt awful but I couldn't commit myself. "I'm sorry ladies but I don't think I can give any practical help; I can't leave Olive to manage the tearoom on her own for long, we're too busy at the moment."

"That's fine, Harriet," said Adele, "we understand and we do have a few volunteers already."

"As soon as we have everywhere clean," went on Wanda, "Fred and his team will start the painting and with a bit of luck that will be finished to allow it time to dry before the event."

"Any questions?" asked Adele.

"No," said the rest of us together.

"Then I declare the meeting closed."

I was the first to stand up. "If you'll excuse me ladies, I need to get back to work but please feel free to stay and chat as long as you like."

Olive was waiting for me when I came downstairs. "That didn't take long," she said.

"No," I said with a smile. "Adele and Wanda have everything under control."

"No surprise there then."

A summons from Adele wasn't easily ignored and her trusty workforce had the hall ready for painting by the end of the day. Fred had suggested that they start the redecorating

on the Saturday morning, partly to allow everything to dry
out but also that was when most of his accrued team had free
time. Vincent had offered his services but I was working and
for once I was glad it wasn't my day off because painting and
decorating had never been my thing and I was happy for an
excuse to be out of the way.

At the end of the day I decided to call in at the hall on my
way home. I was curious to see how they were getting on,
with a bit of luck they might have finished. When I pulled up
in the car park I could see the lights were still on so they
were still there but when I walked in I could tell they were
packing up, job finished. I was impressed. I hadn't realised
how shabby the hall had become but now it was sparkling
like a new pin. The walls had been painted in a very pale
grey emulsion and the woodwork in a deep blue gloss. I
don't know who had picked the colour scheme but I
approved.

Adele was there of course, supervising the workers and as
soon as she spotted me she came straight over. "Haven't they
done a good job, Harriet?"

"They certainly have," I said, scanning the room for a
particular face.

"If you're looking for Vincent, I think he's up in the loft
putting the ladders away."

"Oh, right," I said, although he wasn't who I was looking
for but at that moment Vincent appeared at the top of the loft
ladder followed by Carrie and Fred.

"Hi Mum, were you looking for me?"

"Yes," I lied. "I was wondering if you were nearly ready
to come home for dinner."

"Well actually," he said, "I was going to ring you; a few of us are going to the pub for a bite to eat and a drink, d'you want to come?"

I was tempted but I was quite tired and ready for home so I said "Thank you for asking but I'll give it a miss. Is Dave not here?"

"He was but he left about an hour ago. He had a phone call and said he needed to go."

"Harriet?"

I turned at the sound of a familiar voice. "Hello Norman, did you get roped in to help?"

"Yes but I'm glad to see you. I want to ask you something."

"Oh right, go ahead."

"Olive and I are celebrating our Ruby Wedding anniversary in January and I would like to take her on holiday if she can have the time off."

"Oh Norman, of course she can. Where are you taking her?"

"I've not decided yet but hopefully somewhere warm."

"How lovely, does she know?"

"Not yet so don't say anything, I want it to be a surprise."

"My lips are sealed."

We were interrupted by the sound of Adele's voice. "If everyone is ready can we make our way out of the hall so I can lock up?"

We all did as we were bid and I walked over to my car. I looked for Vincent to say goodbye but he was deep in conversation with Carrie as they walked towards his van together. Curiosity overwhelmed me and once behind the steering wheel I watched as Vincent held open the passenger door to his van to allow Carrie to climb inside. 'Now that's interesting' I thought.

I was sitting in my dressing gown in front of the fire when Vincent came home. His face was wreathed in smiles; he stopped short when he saw me. "You haven't been waiting up for me, have you , Mum?"

"No, love, I was just sitting here trying to persuade myself to get up and go to bed."

"I don't think I'll be long myself," he said, "I'm shattered.

"Did Carrie get home alright?" I asked innocently.

"Yes she came to the pub with us and then I dropped her off at home."

"That was kind of you."

He shrugged his shoulders. "She's a friend and it was on my way."

I stood up and kissed him on the cheek; I was too tired to ask anything else. "Goodnight son," I said.

"Goodnight Mum."

Chapter Nineteen

Olive was bursting with news when she arrived for work on Monday morning. "You'll never guess what that Norman's gone and done."

I thought I might have an inkling but didn't let on. "What?" I said with the right amount of expectancy.

"He's only gone and booked us on a Caribbean cruise."

"Wow," I said, genuinely surprised. "When are you going?"

"The beginning of January, that's if I can have the time off."

I frowned and pretended to consider but then I grinned. "Of course you can have the time off."

She heaved a sigh of relief. "I told Norman he should have let me ask you first before booking but he said he wanted it to be a surprise. It's our Ruby Wedding anniversary, you see, on the sixteenth of January."

I pretended to be surprised again. "You never said anything."

"To be honest, I'd forgotten and was shocked that Norman had remembered."

"I do believe he's an old romantic at heart," I said, smiling.

"I know," she said, her eyes wide in wonderment. "Who'd have thought it?"

She went into the kitchen to hang her coat up and I couldn't resist a little chuckle behind her back. 'Good on you, Norman,' I thought.

I got my second surprise of the morning, shortly afterwards, when Dave Kenyon walked through the door. "Good morning," I said, "have I missed a day? Is it Tuesday?"

"Don't be cheeky," he said with a smile. "I am allowed to come in for a coffee anytime aren't I?"

"That's what we're here for," I said, matching his smile, "and it's a pleasure to see you."

He glanced around the tea room, we hadn't started to get busy yet. "I don't suppose you've time for a chat."

Right on cue Olive walked out of the kitchen. "Of course she has. Why don't you both sit down and I'll bring you some drinks over."

I followed Dave to an empty table and when we sat down he couldn't hold on to his news any longer. "I've found my son."

"That's amazing! How? When?"

"You remember I told you I'd hired a private detective?"

"Yes."

"He rang me on Saturday to say he had news and he came round to the house."

"Is that why you left the village hall early; Vincent said you'd had a phone call."

"Yes. He'd managed to trace my ex-wife who'd remarried and emigrated to Australia with my son."

"Oh," I didn't know if this was good news or bad.

"He found out that George has recently got married himself and he was able to give me his address."

"That's brilliant," I said, relieved that it was good news after all.

"I spent most of yesterday composing a letter. I must have ripped it up and started again twenty times but in the end I kept it simple and included my address, telephone number and email address for good measure."

"Have you posted it?"

"Yes, I called at the post office on my way here."

"How long will it take to get to him?"

His face dropped. "I don't know. I didn't think to ask."

"Perhaps it's as well because otherwise you'd be tracking it in your mind and if you didn't get a reply by return of post you'd be thinking the worst."

"That's a point. My fingernails are nearly down to the bone already as it is."

I couldn't help it, I had to say what was in my mind. "What if he doesn't reply?"

He gave a wry smile. "I've thought of that and I would try again but if he doesn't want to get in touch there's nothing much I can do about it."

"You could look for him on facebook," I suggested.

"Oh yes," he said as if a light bulb had come on over his head. "I hadn't thought of that. I do have an account but I use it mainly for business."

"Also," I said, "you might need to be patient. It may take him time to come to terms with it and make a decision whether or not to write back."

He nodded in agreement. "His mother has probably painted a not too favourable picture of me and he might decide he wants nothing to do with me."

"That's a possibility you might have to face up to," I said. "But on the other hand you're still his father and he might be curious about you, if nothing else."

His smile returned. "I knew you'd be the right person to talk to about this; you have the ability to see both sides of a situation."

"It's much easier when it's someone else's situation," I said, "but not so easy when it's your own."

"Well perhaps I'll be able to return the favour some day."

"I'll hold you to that."

Olive came over with our drinks. "Sorry I've been a while, we had a mini rush on."

I felt guilty. "Sorry, Olive, do you need me to come and help?"

"No, it's nothing I can't handle, you enjoy your drink."

When Dave stayed for his chat after the book club, the next day, I didn't bring up the subject of his son as it was much too early for him to expect a reply. Instead I brought up the subject of the table top sale.

"Will You be there on Saturday?" I asked.

"Yes, I've been roped in as a general dogsbody and to help Brian with the Tombola. I'm also down to set up the tables on Friday night."

"I think Vincent is helping with that as well."

He gave a chuckle. "Yes, that's my doing. He's becoming my regular sidekick."

"Is he *your* Tonto now then?"

He laughed, remembering one of our earlier conversations. "I suppose he is, which means I'm promoted to the Lone Ranger."

"You'll be needing a white hat then." I suggested.

"As long as it doesn't come with a white horse; I never learned to ride."

We both broke into peals of laughter but we were interrupted by Olive. "I'm sorry to gatecrash the party but I'm off home."

"Thanks Olive," I said, "I'll put the closed sign on the door and when everyone has left I'll lock the door."

"Okay, see you tomorrow. See you, Dave."

"Bye Olive," we answered together.

When the door closed behind her the couple sitting at the only other occupied table left as well. As I stood up to lock the door behind them Dave said "How long will it take you to close up?"

"About half an hour or so. Why?"

"I wondered if you'd like to come out for a drink and something to eat with me; I don't feel like going home because I'll only be turning you know what over in my mind and coming up with worst case scenarios."

"So in other words I'd be doing a good deed by taking your mind off it?"

"Precisely."

"Then it would be churlish of me to refuse but let me phone Vincent first in case he's started to prepare something."

I rang his mobile number. "Hi Mum, that's a coincidence I was just about to ring you."

"Oh right, what for?"

"Would you mind eating on your own tonight? I've arranged to go out."

"No, in fact that's why *I* was ringing *you*. Dave has asked me to go out for something to eat with him."

He laughed down the phone. "That's worked out well then, see you later."

The phone went dead before I could reply. I must have frowned because Dave asked "Is something the matter?"

"Not really, he just ended the call quite abruptly that's all."

"But he's okay with you going out with me?"

"Oh yes, apparently he's going out as well."

"Perfect," said Dave. "Now tell me what I can do to help so we can be out of here as soon as possible because I'm starving."

I gave him a list of jobs and working together we were locking up twenty minutes later. It was decided that Dave would follow me home so that I could leave my car and we'd go in his. We ended up at a lovely pub/restaurant set back from the road. It was a pity it was dark because I was sure the surrounding countryside would be breathtaking in daylight. I thought it would be lovely to come on a warm summer's day and eat at one of the outside tables. There were lots of vehicles in the car park but the pub had more than one dining room so we had no trouble getting a table.

It was all waitress service so we could relax while we looked over the menu and decided what to eat and then have it brought to you without having to leave the comfort of your seats. When we'd finished our main course, Dave left me looking at the dessert menu while he went off the find the 'Gents'. He was gone a while and when he came back he was rubbing his chin as if in thought. "What's the matter?" I asked.

"Nothing really, I suppose but when I went into the other room to look for the toilets I spotted Vincent sitting at one of the tables in there."

"My Vincent?"

"Yes."

I started to get up to go and speak to him but Dave grabbed my hand. "Who did he say he was going out with?"

"He didn't. Why, who is he with?"

"Carrie."

"Carrie? Just the two of them?"

Dave nodded and smiled. "I'm only thinking that if he'd wanted you to know who he was meeting he would have told you and he might not be that happy to see you."

"You're right," I said. "I take it he didn't see you."

"I don't think so. It looked as if neither of them could see anyone but each other."

I gave a broad grin. "Best not to disturb them then."

"My thoughts exactly."

"I'd been home for about an hour when Vincent rolled in. "Have you had a nice time?" I asked.

"Yes, lovely. And you?"

"Oh yes I had a really good time."

I was tempted to ask where he'd been but he might have asked me the same and I didn't want him to know we'd been in the same restaurant. I didn't want to lie to him either or force him into telling me his secret. If he wanted me to know he was seeing Carrie, he would tell me in his own good time and I was content to wait.

The next night we went to the pub quiz as usual and I sat back and watched for any interaction between Vincent and Carrie but they didn't act any differently towards each other than they had previously. I offered to go for the quiz paper and met up with Dave at the table.

"Has Vincent said anything?" he asked.

"No and I haven't asked. What about you?"

"Not a dicky bird and I've been with him for most of the day."

"We'll have to watch this space then."

"Harriet, I can't believe you haven't dropped hints or quizzed him about it, if you'll pardon the pun," he said waving his question sheet.

"I've told you before, I don't interfere in the lives of my children. If there's anything to tell he'll come out with it when he's ready."

"I don't think I've ever met a woman like you before," he said, shaking his head.

"That's because I'm unique," I said before swanning off back to my table. I could hear him chuckling behind my back.

Chapter Twenty

After locking up the tearoom on Friday evening I drove round to the village hall to help with setting out the tables. Adele and Wanda were already there and had their heads together over a large sheet of paper, laid out on the stage. They must have heard my footsteps when I came through the door because they turned as one to look at me. "Ah, Harriet," said Adele, "we're looking at the floor plan for the tables and we've allocated you three tables next to the serving hatch from the kitchen. Will that be enough?"

"Probably," I replied. "I can get six chairs around each table but if there are any spare, another one would help."

"We'll see what we can do." she said.

Shortly afterwards, other people started to arrive, Dave and Vincent among them. The aim of tonight was to set out the tables and chairs and put names on the tables. The stallholders were coming in early the next morning to put out their wares. There was a commotion at the door and heads turned to see Fred and Kathleen Thomas entering the hall carrying one of Fred's pasting tables. Adele marched up to them. "What on earth is this?"

"Wanda said you might be short of tables," said Kathleen, "so I thought that if I brought this for the knitting group to use, it would help."

Adele turned on her heel to face an approaching Wanda. "Before you explode, Adele, I did say Kathleen could bring it."

"But it's larger than the other tables," said a red faced Adele, "and it will upset the floor plan!"

"No it won't," argued Wanda, "there's plenty of room and it means Harriet can have the extra table she wanted."

Realising everyone was looking at her, Adele composed herself and with a brief nod, returned to what she was doing. "Right, Kathleen," said Wanda, "I'll show you where to set it up."

There was a brief uncomfortable silence but then everyone got on with what they'd come to do. Once my tables were in place, I covered them with the white cloths I'd brought with me. I placed several coasters on each table and a small vase in the centre; Olive was going to bring some fresh flowers to put in them, in the morning. As I was finishing, Vincent came over to me. "Can you give me a lift back, Mum? I left my van at home and came in with Dave.

"Of course. I'm nearly ready if you are."

We waved goodbye, shouting "See you in the morning," as we left the hall, but as we were crossing the car park I heard someone call my name. I turned to see Dave hurrying after us. I gave Vincent the car keys and waited for Dave to catch up. "I wanted to let you know that I've heard from my son."

"That's wonderful," I replied. "When?"

"He sent me an email asking me if I used social media and if so, to send him a friend request. I did it this morning."

"Oh Dave, I'm so pleased for you. Let me know how you get on."

"I will. See you tomorrow."

When I got into the car Vincent didn't ask what Dave had wanted. Perhaps he'd inherited my policy of non-interference.

After a bit of discussion, Vincent and I decided it would be better to use his van to transport everything I needed to the hall, so early next morning he drove me to the tea room to load up. He helped me carry out packets of bacon, sausages, cooked meats along with the bread rolls and loaves of bread and tubs of butter I'd need to make sandwiches. I'd baked a couple of large Quiches and a multitude of cakes and pastries as well. As promised, before I left, I placed a sign on the door stating we were closed but directing people to the village hall if they wanted refreshments.

The hall was already a hive of activity when we arrived but luckily Olive and Sophie were waiting for us to help unload the van and carry things into the kitchen. Brad was also there but Olive had 'loaned' him to Dorothy Green to help her carry in her boxes of second hand books. When we'd got everything inside Vincent left us to it while he went to offer his services to anyone else who might need a hand.

Olive had had the foresight to switch on the fridge, the warming oven and the hot water boiler when she arrived but it was a little too early to start cooking so I took a moment to look around the room and was pleasantly surprised at the number of stalls being set up.

The Guides and Brownies had a large Teddy Bear sporting a pair of striped pyjamas and bed cap. They had a large sheet of card at the side with lots of names on for people to pick from. Whoever picked the winning name won the teddy. The Cubs and Scouts were running a White Elephant stall and Belinda Quayle was setting up a second hand toy stall. The proceeds of these stalls were being donated to the hall fund.

The Art Group, the Knitting Circle and the Cardmaking Group each had stalls displaying and hopefully selling some of the things their members had created. Ida Jamieson was selling a myriad selection of Christmas goods from stockings to mince pies, Alice Darbyshire from Edderbrook farm had a selection of her home made preserves. Nell Unsworth had her own stall selling and taking orders for items of pottery and there were others selling Handmade Christmas decorations, Home Brew and Farmhouse cheeses.

Brian Kenyon, on his own for the moment, was setting up the Tombola and next to him was Wanda Barraclough laying out the prizes for her big raffle; her table was laden with donations from most of the local businesses and farms. My eyes finally came to rest on the stall I was looking for. Carrie was busy displaying her jewellery and Vincent was helping by setting out the cuddly toys her grandmother had made. I couldn't resist going over. "Hello Carrie, is Amy not coming with you?"

She looked up at me and I was amused to see her blush as she glanced at Vincent. "Mum's bringing her in later. She doesn't do early mornings at this time of year so I said I could manage to set up without her. Vincent offered to give me a hand."

"So I see," I said, smiling. "He's good like that, my son."

I left them to it and walked back towards the kitchen. Sophie was buttering bread rolls for Olive who had put bacon and sausages into a large frying pan on the hob of the oven. She was engrossed in turning the sausage, or so I thought but you should never underestimate the woman who misses nothing. "Your Vincent seems to be getting quite friendly with young Carrie," she said, not taking her eyes from the pan.

"We've been going to the quiz nights at the pub with Carrie and her family, as you know, and that's how they've become friends.

She looked up. "I hope there isn't something you're not telling me," she said.

"You know as much as me," I lied, "if there's anything more to it, Vincent has said nothing to me."

"Haven't you asked him?"

"No, I haven't, honestly you're as bad as Dave?"

"So he's noticed something as well?"

I could have bitten out my tongue. "There is nothing to notice."

"They'd make a good couple though," she said, wistfully.

I had to agree but I wasn't going to say so; instead I said, "what will be will be and it's no use speculating."

She pointed the fork she was using at me. "You can be really infuriating sometimes, Harriet Jones,."

"That makes two of us then, Olive Parker and your sausages are burning."

We both looked round as Sophie began to laugh. "What?" we asked together.

"You two are like a double act, you should be on the stage."

We were saved from answering by Adele calling for attention in the hall and announcing that the doors were going to be opened to the public.

"Action stations!" declared Brad, bursting into the kitchen. "The hungry mob is about to descend on us."

He wasn't wrong. As people poured into the hall most of them made straight for the stalls but some decided to avoid the crush by having something to eat and drink first, including Hilda and Rita Yardley. The Yardleys were elderly twin sisters who were two of my most regular customers and had become dear friends. They sat at one of the tables and waved to me.

"Hello Rita, Hello Hilda, someone will be out in a minute," I called.

Other tables were filling up as well so Brad and Sophie went out to take orders while Olive and I did the cooking. I'd put menus on the table when I first came in. We were kept steadily busy for the next couple of hours but because there were four of us, as it approached lunchtime we were able to take it in turns to have a break. Besides having something to eat, it gave us a chance to look at the stalls.

I waited until last and went to find Vincent who was now sitting at the Tombola stall with Brian and Dave Kenyon. "Have you had any lunch?" I asked him.

"I had a bacon roll first thing," he said, "why?"

"I'm going to take a break and wondered if you wanted to join me."

He looked at his watch. "Yes, I might as well," he said.

"You go and find us somewhere to sit and I'll get the food, my treat."

I noticed he glanced towards Carrie's stall but she and Amy were chatting to Millie, Carrie's mum, who had got them a takeaway from the kitchen. "Is everything okay?" I asked.

He turned to me. "Yes, fine. I'll have a ham salad roll and a piece of cake please."

"Coming up."

Quite a few people had started to drift off home by this time but there were still a few newcomers coming through the door, probably leaving it later to avoid the crush. I was sitting, facing the door and nearly dropped my fruit scone when I recognised a face I hadn't expected to see. I tapped Vincent on the arm and nodded towards the person making their way towards us. "Ah there you are," she said.

"Elaine? What are you doing here?" asked Vincent.

"That's a nice welcome," she said. "I've come to see you of course."

"Are the boys with you?" he said, looking past her hopefully.

"No, Malcolm, their dad, has got them for the weekend."

I wondered if she realised how cruel those words might sound to Vincent but knew that even if she did, she wouldn't care. She was obviously after something but whatever it was, she wouldn't want to ask in front of me so I pushed my scone to one side and said "Why don't you sit down and I'll get you a cup of tea."

"Thank you, Harriet, but could I have coffee, white, no sugar."

"Who's that with Vincent?" asked Olive when I went into the kitchen.

"His ex!"

"That's Elaine? What does *she* want?"

"I don't know but I aim to find out."

I took her the coffee and left them alone but when I went back into the kitchen I hovered around the serving hatch so I could eavesdrop on their conversation. Elaine was speaking.

"I went to your mum's house first but when you weren't there I tried the tea room and saw the notice on the door."

"Well, you couldn't have been just passing so why *are* you here?"

"I was missing you and I thought that if I came up you might like to take me out to dinner. There are some lovely pubs around here that have accommodation. I thought if we booked a room we could both have a drink…"

My heart was literally in my throat as I waited for his reply.

"I'm sorry, Elaine, but I don't know what time I'll get away from here. When the sale closes we'll have to put all the tables away and tidy up. It might get late."

"I don't mind waiting," she said.

At this point I could bear it no longer. I dashed out of the kitchen on the pretence of retrieving my half eaten scone, which I could have quite easily smashed in her face. Instead I remained outwardly calm and spoke to Vincent. "By the way, I forgot to mention that Olive and Norman have invited a few of us, including you round to their house when we leave here. I think Norman has prepared something because he knows how tired we'll be."

"That's really good of him," said Vincent, catching on straight away. "I'm sorry Elaine, I'm already booked."

"I could come with you," she said.

"I'm sorry," I said but there isn't room. Olive's house is only small and they've only catered for so many."

Her face looked as if she'd just swallowed a wasp but she wasn't beaten yet. "That's a shame," she said, "I was hoping to discuss arrangements for Christmas."

By the hopeful look on his face she must have thought she had him but he said "We can talk about it now. Can I see the boys? Perhaps I could bring them here for a couple of days before they go back to school."

"I'm sorry that won't be possible," she said, reaching for his hand across the table. Malcolm is taking them on holiday for the whole two weeks but I thought you might like to come over and spend it with me. Just the two of us."

I've never seen Vincent grow so angry so quickly but he snatched his hand away and gave her a look full of hatred but without raising his voice he said, "So, that's it. You don't want to spend Christmas on your own so you thought you'd make do with me for company and I'd be so desperate that I'd come running. Well, I've got news for you, I'm not *that* desperate and I've already made plans which don't include you!"

She drew back as if she'd been slapped; this retaliation was so out of character for Vincent but she soon recovered. "If that's how you feel, you can forget about ever seeing the boys again."

"I think I'd already reached that conclusion; you never had any intention of letting me see them but they were the carrot that you could dangle before me. So it will be no surprise when I cancel the direct debit I've been paying into your bank account for them."

"You can't do that," she pleaded. "I rely on that money."

"Then you'd better ask Malcolm to cover it because as you keep reminding me *he's* their *real* father, not me."

"In that case, I might as well go," she said.

"Don't let *us* keep you," said Vincent.

When she didn't make a move, I said "I think it might be better if you set off now, the days are short at this time of year and you don't want to be driving along unfamiliar country roads in the dark."

If looks could kill, as they say, I would have dropped dead on the spot but with as much dignity as she could muster she stood up and left the hall without a backward glance. I watched her go and then turned to Vincent who was sitting with his elbows on the table, resting his head in his hands. "Are you alright, son?" I asked.

He looked up at me and nodded. "If anything I feel relieved; I'll miss the boys terribly but if that's the price I have to pay to be rid of their mother, I'll learn to live with it."

I placed my hand on his shoulder. "For what it's worth," I said, "I think you've done the right thing. It needed a complete break to allow you to get on with your life."

He put his hand on mine. "I love you, Mum."

"I love you too, Son."

Although neither Vincent nor Elaine had raised their voice the altercation had not gone unnoticed. Olive had heard every word from her position at the serving hatch but for once kept her opinions to herself, at least for the moment. It was Dave who took me to one side when Vincent went over to sit with Carrie; Millie had taken Amy home and she was on her own on the stall.

"I'm sorry," said Dave, "I wasn't eavesdropping but I couldn't help overhearing most of that; is Vincent okay?"

"If he's not, at the moment," I said, "he will be and as far as I'm concerned he's better off out of it."

"Mm," he said, "is it true you've been invited to Olive's for supper?"

"No but I wasn't going to allow Elaine to guilt trip Vincent into taking her out and, heaven forbid, spend the night with her. Why are you smiling?"

"What happened to the rule of non-interference?"

"Some rules need to be broken in an emergency," I said with a smile.

"Anyway," he said, nodding towards Carrie's stall, "I know someone who, with a bit of luck, might be exactly what he needs to help him get over this."

I followed his gaze. "I hope so, Dave, I really hope so."

I looked at my watch, it was three thirty and there were few customers left in the hall so most of the stallholders were starting to cash up. I took my leave of Dave and went into the kitchen to do the same but Olive had already started. "Have you got the receipts for the food?" she asked.

"Yes," I said, "They're in my purse. I'll hand them in with the money we've taken and Adele will reimburse me."

I was impressed with the profit we'd made and felt we'd done our bit for the cause. At four o'clock, on the dot, Adele stood up and declared the sale closed. She was happy to announce that the total raised so far was over two thousand pounds but there was still money to come in. The news was accepted with a round of applause before the stallholders started to pack up.

We had almost sold out; there were a few sandwiches and small cakes left so with Olive's agreement I told Brad and Sophie to share them and take them home. I was folding up the tablecloths when Vincent came over.

"Mum, I hope you don't mind but I've asked Dave to give you a lift home; I've promised Carrie to help her pack up and then drop her off at her gran's with the stuff that's left."

"Did Carrie not bring her car? How did she get the stuff here?"

"Her mum brought her this morning. Carrie doesn't have a car of her own but Millie left early when Amy started to get tired."

"Then if Dave doesn't mind, I'm happy with that."

"Thanks, Mum."

When I was ready to leave, Dave came up to me. "I believe I'm your taxi home."

"Does that mean you intend to charge me for the ride?" I said in mock disbelief.

"Absolutely," he said, "but I don't want money."

"Excuse me, what other payment had you in mind?"

He laughed out loud. "Only your company; will you let me take you out to supper?"

"No," I said, causing him to frown, "but I will come with you for something to eat."

"What's the difference?"

"If you take me out then I expect you to pick up the bill but if I accompany you, we can go halves."

He shook his head as he smiled. "You're a very obstinate woman, Harriet Jones, but I don't mind who pays as long as we eat."

"Do you mind if we call at the cafe on the way so I can drop some stuff off, it's just the tablecloths and vases mainly but there are some other odds and ends."

"Not at all."

He helped me carry the things to the car and as we were setting off I remembered something. "By the way, who won you in the raffle?"

I could see his smile, even in the dark. "The Misses Yardley; are you disappointed it wasn't you?"

"Not really," I said, "I was so busy I never got around to buying a ticket."

"Charming."

It was only after we'd eaten that he told me his news. "I've had a message from George and we're having a face to face call in the morning."

"That's brilliant," I said. "What time?"

"Nine thirty; he's ten hours ahead of me so it will be evening for him."

"Are you excited?"

"Yes and extremely nervous. What if he doesn't like me?"

"He will," I said with confidence.

Chapter Twenty One

I was in bed when Vincent came home so I didn't see him until the following morning at breakfast. I'd decided to close the tearoom today so we could all have a rest after being so busy at the sale. Vincent was having a lie in but I tempted him out of his bed with the smell of bacon, cooking. "That smells good, Mum," he said. He was still in his pyjamas and looked half asleep.

"Sit yourself down," I said, "It's nearly ready."

I'd cooked us both a Full English and we both did justice to it. When I got up to do the dishes, Vincent said, "Leave those, Mum, I'll do them but I want to talk to you first."

"Okay," I said, sitting back down. "What's on your mind?"

"After the events of yesterday it's pretty obvious that Elaine and I are over for good."

"I would agree with you there."

He cleared his throat as he struggled with the next bit. "One of the reasons I'm not as bothered about that as I might have been is that I've met someone else."

I couldn't help the smile spreading across my face. "Really?"

He looked at me suspiciously. "You've guessed, haven't you? It's Carrie."

"Well, I could see you were getting quite friendly but I knew you would tell me if there was something I should know."

"You don't mind?"

"Why on earth should I mind?"

"Because it's so soon after my break up with Elaine that I thought you might think I'm on the rebound."

"I hope that's not the only reason you've taken a shine to Carrie," I said. "She's a lovely girl and I wouldn't want her to get hurt."

"No, I really like her. We get on so well and I enjoy her company immensely. Every time I leave her, I can't wait to see her again."

"Then I couldn't be happier for you."

"That's not everything though and you might not be as happy about the next bit."

A cold hand gripped my happy feeling. "What is it?" I asked.

"I think I'd like to settle down here; I've started to get regular work and I'm starting to feel at home in the area."

The cold hand loosened its grip. "That's absolutely great, why might I not be happy about it?"

"I think It's time I found a place of my own."

"Oh, I see."

He reached out and took my hand. "I've loved staying with you, Mum, but it was never meant to be permanent; it gave me the breathing space I needed while I came to terms with things and considered my future and I'm grateful for that."

"Are you and Carrie planning to move in together?"

He smiled and shook his head. "It's much too early for that. As I said, I really like her and I think she feels the same way about me but cohabiting is a long way off. Besides, I think that if a woman came to live with me again, I'd prefer us to get married first; I would feel more secure and if things did go wrong at least I wouldn't lose my children."

I thought about Dave's situation but didn't want to burst Vincent's bubble, instead I said "Can you afford a place of your own?"

"I can now I'm not sending money to Elaine. I'm earning quite well and there's plenty of work in the pipeline; of course it would have to be something small at first, a flat or something."

"Then I'm happy for you. I've loved having you here but I understand your need for independence and hopefully you'll be able to find somewhere not too far away from me."

"Besides," he said, carrying the plates to the sink, "you don't want a grown up son cramping your own style."

"What d'you mean?"

He looked at me and grinned. "Come off it, Mum, don't think I haven't noticed the chemistry between you and Dave Kenyon."

I started to protest but he put the plates down and hugged me. "Go for it, Mum, Dad's been gone a long time and you deserve to be happy. He'd want that too."

When he released me from his arms I left him to the washing up and made myself comfortable in the armchair in the lounge. I picked up my book but couldn't concentrate on reading; I kept thinking about what Vincent had said. Perhaps it was time for me to own up to myself how I really felt about Dave, and Vincent was right, I did deserve to be happy.

Two hours later the man in question was knocking on my front door. Vincent was on his way out to meet Carrie and let him in. I heard him tell Dave to go through to the living room.

"Hello," I said, putting a marker in my book and placing it on the coffee table in front of me, "This is a nice surprise."

He glanced towards the book. "I'm not disturbing you, am I?"

"Not at all, I'm glad for the company, sit down."

"I went to the tea room and then remembered you were closed today."

"I'm glad you came," I said. "How did facetime go with George?"

His face lit up with a beaming smile. "Better than I could ever have expected."

I was getting as excited as he was. "Go on, tell me everything."

"I think we both felt a bit awkward at first but then I asked him why he'd gone to live in Australia. He said that after the divorce his mum had met and married an Australian. He was a professional rugby player and when his contract was up with the club he was playing for he signed for one back in Australia and they all moved out there."

"Was he happy with that? George, I mean."

"He was only a child and I suppose it was an adventure but he seems to be settled there. He said his mum and stepdad had two more children so he has a half brother and a half sister."

"How did he feel about you getting in touch?"

"He was delighted. He said his stepfather had never treated him any differently from his own children and he loved him for it but he'd always known that his birth father was out there somewhere. He said that when he grew up he wanted to find me but didn't know how his mum would feel about it."

"Did he know why you'd got divorced?"

"No, I'll give Tina her due, she never said anything that might turn him against me and I wouldn't have blamed her if she had."

"Did you tell him?"

"Yes. I was upfront and told him the truth. I told him I wasn't proud of my behaviour and he thanked me for being honest with him but said it was all in the past and we should start with a clean sheet."

I was starting to really like this young man. "That was lovely of him. Does his mum know you've made contact with him?"

"Yes, he felt he should ask her permission before he got back to me but she was fine about it. Apparently she's been really happy in her second marriage so I probably did her a favour."

I had to smile at the downcast look that accompanied this last remark. "Don't you think *you* could have made her happy?"

"Not back then. We were married quite young before I was really ready to settle down but Tina was pregnant and in those days it was what was expected of us."

"And you never met anyone else, later on?"

A twinkle came into his eye. "I've had my flirtations but I never met anyone I cared about enough to want to get serious with." He looked me in the eye. "That is until now."

My heart flipped, did a double somersault and jumped up and down in my chest. I began to feel warm all over. "Do you mean me?"

"Yes, Harriet, I mean you. Have I overstepped the mark?"

I could feel my face glowing. "No you haven't overstepped the mark. I feel the same way about you."

He heaved a deep sigh. "Thank goodness for that. I felt like a schoolboy asking his date to the prom."

I smiled at the thought. "We're not exactly teenagers," I said.

"No, but we're not in our dotage either."

"That's true," I said.

We both laughed but then became a little self-conscious with each other. I broke the ice in the only way I knew how. "Shall I put the kettle on?"

"No," he said, "I'm on too much of a high to stay in; d'you fancy a drive in the country, a bit of a walk and then dinner, somewhere cosy?"

"Yes," I said immediately. "I fancy that very much."

"Then let's do it; it will be our first proper date."

We drove through some beautiful countryside but I hardly saw any of it as all I could think of was the man beside me in the driving seat. Vincent would be cock a hoop when he heard about the development in mine and Dave's relationship and I could see a 'told you so' coming my way.

We finally parked up in Ambleside. The sun was shining but a cold wind was blowing off Lake Windermere. We'd come prepared with our thick winter coats but when Dave took hold of my hand as we began our walk, my own internal central heating sparked up and gave me a warm feeling all through my body.

During the course of the afternoon Dave told me that he and Geaorge had arranged another facetime next week at the same time and I told him Vincent's news. "Wow," he said, "things are really moving on."

We decided to stay in Ambleside for dinner and chose one of the town's many eating establishments. After we'd eaten we sat for a while in easy conversation and enjoyed each other's company. It was late in the evening when Dave finally dropped me off   at home; he declined my invitation to come in for a coffee as he had an early start the following day but as I made to open the car door, he stopped me. "Harriet, may I kiss you?"

"I thought you'd never ask," I said.

Chapter Twenty Two

I was bursting to tell Olive all of my news the next morning; I knew she'd be another who would be smug, saying she'd been right all along about both relationships but I also knew she'd be really happy for me. Before she arrived for work, however, I had a visitor. Adele Kenyon came through the door as if she was walking on air.

"Harriet, I couldn't wait to tell you, the final total raised by the sale was over three thousand pounds."

"That's amazing," I said, "that should cover the rent of the shop for quite a few weeks until it starts to make money."

"I know," she said, "I'm sorry I can't stay longer but if you could contact Mrs. Phillips and negotiate a price then I can call a meeting to discuss the way forward."

Before I could agree she bounced out of the cafe, almost colliding with Olive in the doorway. After a brief apology she hurried away.

"My, she's in a good mood," said Olive.

"Yes, hurry up and take your coat off while I make us a coffee; I've got a lot to tell you."

She shot into the kitchen like a bullet from a gun; there was nothing she liked more than a good gossip. We had a little over an hour before the creative writing group was due and no other customers at the moment so we could chat in comfort. I didn't tell Olive about Dave's contact with his son as I felt it wasn't my place but when I'd finished giving her the rest of the news she looked like she was going to explode with glee.

"Oh Harriet, I'm so thrilled about all of it; the money, Vincent and Carrie and you and Dave; I feel like dancing round the tables." Suddenly she started laughing.

"What's tickling you?" I asked.

"I was right all along, wasn't I? You and Dave, Carrie and Vincent; I have a nose for these things."

"Well your surname *is* Parker."

I was going to ask Olive to hold the fort for a short while after lunch so I could go and speak to Clara Phillips but I had no need to because around eleven o'clock the lady herself walked into the tearoom. "Hello, Clara," I said, "I was going to pop round and see you this afternoon."

She seemed quite nervous as she said "Might I have a word with you, Harriet?"

"Yes, of course. Come through to the kitchen and I can be making up sandwiches while we talk."

She sat down at the kitchen table but seemed reluctant to open the conversation so I did. "Is something wrong, Clara?"

"I won't be able to rent you the shop," she blurted out.

I sat down opposite her; this was a blow. "Why ever not?" I asked.

"I didn't go to the table top sale on Saturday because my sister rang me; she'd had a fall."

"Oh no, was she badly hurt?"

She shook her head. "Thankfully not, just a few hefty bruises but nothing broken. It really scared her though; she's two years older than me and was widowed not long after I lost Michael."

"You must have been a great comfort to each other."

"We were and still are, neither of us having been blessed with children. Anyway, she's worried about living on her own in case it happens again so she has asked me to go and live with her."

I thought I knew where this was heading. "So you'll need to sell the shop?"

"Yes and the flat that goes with it because I'll need the money to live on."

An idea was formulating in my brain but I needed time to let it develop so I asked Clara two questions. "Have you had the property valued yet?"

"No, I haven't had time."

"Would you be willing to rent out both properties instead of selling them?"

She paused to give this some thought. "Yes, I would because that would give me a regular income. Why?"

"My son is living with me at the moment but he wants to move out and I think the flat might suit him."

"I would be able to leave most of the furniture for him," she said. "I won't need it at my sister's and I didn't know what I was going to do with it."

Remembering what I'd seen of Claras's decor, I knew it wouldn't exactly be Vincent's cup of tea but he had nothing of his own and it would put him on for the present. "Let me speak to him, Clara, and I'll get back to you."

She stood to leave. "I'd be most grateful if you would, I've told my sister I'll need time to sort things out but the sooner I can move in with her the better."

I waited until after we'd eaten before I broached the subject of Clara's flat with Vincent but when I did, I could tell by his face that he was interested. "Where is it?" he asked.

"It's on the main street in the village, over the gift shop that we want to convert into a charity shop."

"And she's leaving it furnished?"

I pulled a face. "She may take some things with her but she's leaving all the essentials; however, I have to warn you that the decor is lovely but more suited to an elderly lady's home than a young man's bachelor pad."

He chuckled. "Beggars can't be choosers and if the rent is within my budget I'm definitely interested."

"How about I make arrangements with Clara for you to go and have a look at it and you can discuss that with her?"

"Let me know when it's convenient for her and we could go together."

"I will but I've been thinking further ahead."

"Go on," he urged.

"I know you're only just getting back on your feet financially but if and when you could afford to buy it, the property could be a good investment."

"What d'you mean?"

"If you bought the whole property the rent from the shop would help towards the mortgage and if you wanted to move to somewhere bigger in the future you could rent out the flat as a holiday let."

"By the heck, Mum, you've really thought this through."

"I'm being selfish really," I said. "Now I've got you here I intend for you to stay."

He chuckled again. "I've a feeling you might get your way."

Vincent and I went to see Clara the next afternoon and she took us up to the flat. "I wouldn't be charging you extra rent because it's furnished," she said, "because you'd be saving me the bother of selling the furniture or the expense of putting it in storage. Of course you might want to redecorate but that's fine by me."

Vincent then asked about the possibility of buying the property when he was more financially secure. "That would suit me fine." she said.

"Then I think you've got yourself a tenant," said Vincent, shaking her hand.

"I'll ring my solicitor," she said, "to draw up a contract and then everything is done correctly and I'll ring my sister to tell her the good news."

"When were you thinking of moving?" I asked.

"I was planning to close the gift shop after the New Year holiday but under the circumstances I'm going to bring that forward so I can go as soon as possible. It's too far to travel back and forth every day. I'll pack up everything from the shop that I want to take with me but whatever stock is left I'll leave as a donation to the charity shop."

"That's very kind of you," I said. "It also means that we can probably open the charity shop sooner than intended and can start paying you rent."

"There's no rush for that; I have my pension to keep me going and my sister won't let me starve."

Vincent and I were both well satisfied when we took our leave of Clara. When I got back to the tea room the book club was in full swing upstairs. When Dave came down, I thought I'd ask him for Adele's number so I could ring and update her; I'd lost the original piece of paper he'd given me. On the subject of Dave, I'd threatened Olive with all means of torture if she teased him about our relationship but she knew I wouldn't go through with it and I was expecting some embarrassing remarks when he made an appearance. Little did I know that she'd collard him when he first arrived and asked him if she needed to buy a hat.

I rang Adele when I got home. "You've saved me a visit," she said. "I was going to pop in tomorrow to tell you I've arranged a committee meeting for Thursday evening in the hall; we can discuss our next steps then."

Chapter Twenty Three

Vincent and I attended the quiz on Wednesday night as usual but as soon as we arrived it was obvious that Carrie had told her family about her relationship with Vincent and by the looks on their faces they were as happy about it as I was. "Carrie's told us the news," said Millie to Vincent. Carrie had saved him a place next to her and he gave her a hug as he sat down.

"You haven't asked my permission to court my daughter, young man," said Alan, with a straight face."

"My apologies, sir," said Vincent in the same manner. "Do I have your permission?"

"That depends on whether or not you can afford to get the first round in because if you can't, I'm not sure about your prospects."

"Hang on, Alan," said Mille, "he's not asking for her hand in marriage."

"Oh right," said Alan. "I'd better get the drinks then but you can come and help me carry them, Vincent."

Millie shook her head in amusement but when the men had gone to the bar she brought up a subject that had not even crossed my mind yet. "What are you doing for Christmas, Harriet?"

"Gosh, I hadn't even thought about it. Why?"

"Well I presume you'll be closing the cafe so we'd like to invite you and Vincent to come to us for Christmas dinner."

"That's very kind of you. Are you sure?"

"Yes. It will only be Alan and I, Carrie and Terry and Amy, Alan's mum; we've plenty of room for two more."

"In that case I'd love to accept and I'm sure Vincent will feel the same."

She patted my hand. "He does. Carrie's already asked him but he said it was up to you."

I laughed. "So I was an afterthought?"

Millie looked aghast. "Not at all, Carrie's invitation was to the both of you."

"I'm only teasing," I said. "We'd love to come."

Dave was at the quiz with his usual group of friends; apart from Olive and Vincent, I hadn't told anyone about the development in our own relationship. He came over for a brief chat in the interval but because this was what he usually did, it didn't attract any comment. My day off was Saturday, this weekend, and we'd already planned to spend the day together. Vincent would be at the art group which made me wonder if Carrie was aware that she was dating a male model.

For once I was the last to arrive at the committee meeting on Thursday evening; I'd called to see Clara Phillips on my way so I could update the other members on any developments. When I walked into the hall I could feel the optimism in the room as the other ladies chatted amongst themselves and when I took my seat, Adele opened the meeting by announcing the full total of money raised by the table top sale which promoted a round of applause. She then asked if I had any information about the shop.

I began by telling them of the change in Clara's plans and the reason for this but waived away their concerns by assuring them that the rental of the shop could go on as planned. "I've just been to see Clara and she's hoping to move out on Saturday and she will hand the keys over before she goes. This means we can have access to the shop from Sunday."

Wanda Barraclough raised her hand to speak. "Do we have a written contract, Harriet, or just a verbal agreement?"

"We have it in writing," I replied. "Because she's renting out the flat as well, she's had everything drawn up by a solicitor and I have the papers with me; they need to be signed and witnessed."

It went without saying that as chairperson of the committee, Adele would sign and Wanda, as secretary, would witness. Clara had already signed.

"Let's hope," said Adele, "that whoever rents the flat doesn't give us any trouble."

"I can guarantee that he won't," I said, "because it's my son, Vincent."

"Really?" said Nell, "he never said."

"It was only decided a couple of days ago."

"I expect you'll miss him when he moves out," said Dorothy.

I was prevented from answering by Adele, banging her hand on the table, giving everyone a start. "Excuse me ladies but can we leave the general chit chat until after the meeting; there are more important matters we need to discuss."

I could feel my cheeks burning; I felt like a school child being told off for talking in class and glancing at Dorothy, she appeared to feel the same. We exchanged a look and I had to smother the urge to giggle.

"Right then," said Adele, "when do we want to move in?"

"I think the first thing we need to establish," said Nell, "is who is going to run it. Do we have a list of volunteers?"

"A few," said Wanda, taking a list of names out of her folder, "but we need to recruit more."

"I'm sorry but I can't volunteer," said Nell, "I have a business to run and have little enough time off as it is and I expect Harriet will be the same."

"Yes I am," I said.

"You can put my name on the list," said Dorothy, "but I can't do Tuesdays."

Wanda wrote it on the sheet.

"How many days are we going to open?" asked Belinda Quayle.

"That depends on the number of volunteers we get," said Wanda "and what hours they can do."

"I could probably spare a few hours during the week," said Belinda, "when the children are at school."

Wanda wrote this down.

"In my experience," I put in, "we need to be open on weekends if we want to make the most of the tourist trade."

"That's a good point," said Wanda.

"I forgot to say," I went on, "Clara said she will give us the first four weeks rent free to give us time to get it off the ground and she is donating any stock she has left to give us a start."

"That's very generous of her," said Belinda. "I think a thank you card and a bunch of flowers is in order."

"I second that," said Nell.

"Who will sort that out?" asked Adele, looking around the group.

"I will," said Dorothy.

"Thank you," said Adele, "Wanda will reimburse you out of petty cash. Now let's move on to volunteer recruitment."

"I could put a notice up in the window of the tea shop," I offered.

"Good idea, Harriet, thank you and we could put one in the window of the shop itself."

"I'll ask Karl to announce it in church," said Belinda, "and I'll see to it that a notice goes in the church magazine."

"Are you happy for people to contact you, Adele?" asked Wanda.

"Yes as long as my phone number is only given out to people who have a genuine interest, otherwise you open yourself up to all sorts of crank calls like I did when it went on the flyers."

Nobody was brave enough to ask what sort of calls they were even though we were all burning with curiosity."

"We also need to ask for donations," I said, "and we could do with some rails to hang clothing on."

"I'll ask around," said Wanda, "but we could put that on the notices as well."

"I'll ask Vincent to pick up the keys for us when he collects those for the flat," I said. "Who shall I hand them on to?"

"Me," said Adele, before anyone else could answer, "but I'll get another set cut because I think we'll need more than one."

Everyone murmured in agreement.

"Where can people take donations until the shop is open?" asked Dorothy.

"Perhaps you could see to that Wanda," said Adele. "I don't have the space to store anything."

Wanda glared at her. "And you wouldn't want the clutter, I expect."

"Look," I said, "Wanda lives out in the country and people might find it difficult to get to her but I have some space in my storeroom over the cafe and the tea room is pretty central for folks to get to."

"That's a splendid suggestion, Harriet, thank you," said Wanda, shooting a look of pure ice at Adele, whose skin was quite thick enough for it to bounce off.

Vincent was watching television when I got home but looked up when I came in. "You look shattered, Mum," he said.

"I am, it's been a long day."

"I'll put the kettle on, shall I make you something to eat?"

"Thanks but I had something at the cafe before I went to the meeting but I'd love a cup of coffee."

He went into the kitchen and I went into my bedroom to change into my slippers. When I came back, two cups of coffee were on the coffee table but as I settled myself into the armchair I noticed Vincent watching me with a frown on his face."

"What's the matter?"

"You work too hard, Mum. Perhaps I shouldn't move out after all, I could stay here and look after you."

I was really touched by his concern but I had to put him straight. "I *am* tired and I *do* work hard but I'm not yet past it and I'm quite capable of looking after myself."

"I know that but…"

I interrupted him. "I've loved having you here, Vincent, but you have your own life to lead and for that matter, so have I. Don't put yourself on a guilt trip on my account, there's no need."

He smiled. "Well at least I'm not moving far."

"Now *that* I'm really happy about."

Chapter Twenty Four

Clara moved out of the flat on the appointed day; because she wasn't taking much furniture with her it wasn't the onerous task that it might have been. Although neither Clara nor her sister had any children, they had a brother who had two strapping sons and they provided the manpower she needed. Vincent had offered to help but he wasn't really needed. As she had done with the shop, she gave Vincent four weeks before he needed to pay any rent; this gave him time for a touch of redecorating. It also allowed Vincent to take the decision to not move in until after Christmas; which made me very happy.

When word got around about donations for the charity shop, they came in thick and fast and were building up to quite a pile in my storeroom; the only things I couldn't accept were large items of furniture because apart from taking up too much space, there was the physical aspect of getting them up and down the stairs.

Surprisingly it was Dave who managed to acquire the clothing rails we needed. He was working on the refurbishment of a shop in Keswick; it had been a dress shop but had recently been sold to someone who was turning it into a small art gallery. The rails were destined for the skip until Dave, with the owner's permission, rescued them.

Wanda called in the services of her list of volunteers which was beginning to get longer to sort out the donations and transfer them to the shop. They were hoping to open to the public ready for the Christmas holidays. I kept well out of the way, using the genuine excuse that I was too busy. In the past I would probably have offered to help out on my day off but I decided it was time I did something for myself and spent the time with Dave instead.

I was working on the day of the grand opening but Sophie and Brad assured me they could hold the fort while I went across to watch Adele cut the ribbon to declare the shop open. The committee had laid on some glasses of sparkling wine and nibbles for the occasion and there were plenty of prospective customers waiting to partake of the refreshments but also eager to have a nosy around the shop, hoping to pick up a bargain. I left them to it and went back to work, feeling I'd done my duty by showing my face.

The Sunday before Christmas I was waiting for Dave to pick me up; I'd booked us a table for lunch at the local carvery for one o'clock. This would give him plenty of time for his now regular facetime with George. Vincent was going out with Carrie but spotted me waiting at the window. He'd already given me some ribbing about my relationship with Dave; not because he disapproved but because he said he'd known about it all along.

"Waiting for your boyfriend?" he asked, amused.

"I'd hardly call him a boy," I retorted.

"Your man friend then?"

"Yes I am and don't you be cheeky about it."

"I wouldn't dare," he said as he walked past me and into the hall, "but make sure he gets you home for a decent time."

He nipped out of the door and closed it behind him before I could give him a slap and then came and pulled a face at me through the window. "I'll get you later," I shouted through the glass.

He'd only been gone a couple of minutes when Dave pulled up in his red Vauxhall Astra; I waved to him through the window, picked up my coat and bag and left the house. When I settled myself into the passenger seat, he greeted me in the usual manner with a warm smile and a brief kiss. It was only when we'd been driving for a while that I realised he was only going through the motions of listening to my chatter as if his mind was elsewhere.

I waited until we were ensconced in our nice cosy booth before asking him what was wrong. He gave me his usual smile. "By the heck, Harriet, you should have been a detective; nothing gets past you."

I took that as a compliment. "Well you'd better come clean before I shine my interrogation lamp into your eyes.

That made him laugh. "There's no need for that, I was going to tell you anyway." He still hesitated before saying "George has asked me to go over for a visit."

I tried to look more pleased than I felt. "That's lovely, how long for?"

"He wants me to go for a month but I don't know if that's too long. What if we don't get on?"

"Then you can come home but I think it might take you a while to get used to one another before you can start to enjoy each other's company."

"That's what *he* said."

"When does he want you to go?"

"After the New Year holiday; it's summer over there, of course and he'll be on his summer break from work. We'd be able to spend more time together."

"That seems reasonable," I said, "have you told him you'll go?"

"Not yet." He hesitated and then said "I don't suppose you'd like to come with me? I know it's expensive but I can afford to pay for both of us."

That came as a bolt from the blue but no matter what my heart wanted, my mind knew it was impossible. "I'd love to," I said and saw hope gleam in his eyes "but I can't. I couldn't leave the tearoom for so long , especially as Olive will be away for a couple of weeks."

"Could you not close for those two weeks? I know you've said business is quiet at that time."

"It is but I have the groups to consider now and it's not only that; when Olive comes back I'd like to go to my daughters for a couple of days and I was hoping to go and visit Rose."

Dave knew the story of how I met Rose; she'd been a wanderer who I'd discovered in a bad way after she'd had an accident. We'd become friendly and she'd come to stay with me for a while when she came out of hospital. During that time she rediscovered a daughter who'd been given up for adoption as a baby and when she was fully recovered, Rose had gone to live with her in Liverpool. We still kept in touch and Valerie, her daughter, had invited me down for a visit.

He looked really disappointed. "I really want to go and see George but…" He took hold of my hand across the table, "We're only just getting to know one another properly."

"And that's another reason why I shouldn't come with you. You need to concentrate on getting to know your son; I would be in the way of that. He deserves your full attention."

He sighed and nodded his head. "I can see what you mean but I'll miss you."

I squeezed his hand. "And I'll miss you but it's only four weeks and I'll still be here when you get back."

"I hope so," he said, "I'd hate to lose what's growing between us."

I started to giggle. "What?" he asked.

"Nothing," I said, trying to control myself, "only I hope that wasn't a euphemism."

He still looked bewildered and then I almost saw the lightbulb come on over his head and he also laughed. "Harriet Jones, you naughty girl."

Chapter Twenty Five

Vincent finally moved out the day after Boxing Day.
"We'd spent a lovely day on Christmas Day with the
Gordons who'd made us feel part of their family; after lunch
I stayed behind with Millie and Amy to help with the
washing up while the others took advantage of the winter
sunshine to walk off their meal. Millie persuaded Amy to sit
and relax, assuring her that she and I could manage. It was
while we were alone in the kitchen that Millie said "I'm so
pleased for Carrie and Vincent but I was a little worried at
first because I knew Vincent had only just come out of a
relationship and Carrie's last one ended badly; I didn't want
to see her get hurt again."

"I totally understand," I said. "Vincent was really hurt by
his ex partner but I couldn't wish for anyone better than
Carrie to help him get over it and if it helps, he has told me
how much he likes Carrie."

Vincent and I spent Boxing Day together on our own;
normally I would be working but Olive had persuaded me
that they could manage without me while I had some time
with my son. During the morning we had a facetime call
with Naiomi and her family; they'd spent Christmas Day
with Mike's parents.

"I'm so jealous of you, Vincent," said Naiomi, "being able
to spend all this time with Mum; I wish we could be with
you."

"Perhaps next year we could sort something out," I said.

When we'd finished the call Vincent said "Y'know, Mum,
I thought I was happy with Elaine and the boys but being

here with you and meeting Carrie has shown me what happiness can really be like."

I felt the tears prick the back of my eyes. "That's the best Christmas present I could have asked for."

The next day was a bittersweet occasion for both of us; being sad at the parting but looking forward to having our own space again. The consolation being that he wasn't moving far. The actual move didn't take long as he had only got his clothes and personal belongings to transport but I followed him down to the village to make sure, as a mum would, that he had everything he needed. Olive was coming early to open up to give me time to see him settled.

When I was satisfied I kissed him good luck and then left him to it. Before going across to the tea room I looked into the charity shop. It was the first time I'd been in since the opening although I'd been kept up to date with its progress by my customers. Adele was behind the counter. "Hello," I said, "I didn't know you were on the list of volunteers."

There were two other ladies dusting down the items on the shelves, I knew them by sight but didn't know their names. They both looked at me and rolled their eyes.

"I'm not on the list," said Adele, "but I come in as often as I can to ensure that everything is running smoothly."

"To check up on us, more like," whispered one of the ladies.

"Did you have a nice Christmas?" I asked Adele, trying to change the subject.

"Yes, thanks," she said. "Actually I thought Dave might have brought you with him; he spent the day with us and I told him he could ask you."

"He did," I said, "and thank you for the invitation but Vincent and I had already been invited to the Gordons."

"Well perhaps next year, if the two of you are still friendly."

"Yes, perhaps," I said, thinking perhaps not.

As with Vincent, I left them to it; Sophie wasn't due in until later and Olive would be getting busy. She was. She smiled with relief when I walked through the door so I dashed into the kitchen to take off my coat and put on my apron.

Because I'd had Boxing Day off I told Olive she could have New Year's Eve off. This would give her a decent break as we weren't opening on New Year's Day because for the first time in a long time I was going out on New Year's Eve. Dave and I were going to a dinner and dance party at one of the country hotels and had booked rooms so neither of us needed to drive home.

I closed early on that day so I could go home and have a shower and pack my bag; we were getting changed at the hotel. It was a black tie affair and neither of us wanted to travel in our glad rags. My stomach was filled with a whole host of butterflies as I waited for Dave to pick me up; it took me back to my courting days with Eric. At six o'clock he blew his car horn to let me know he was outside and I walked out to the car on legs that quivered like jelly.

After checking in at the hotel we went straight to our rooms to get changed. "Give me a ring when you're ready," said Dave "and I'll call for you." His room was on the same floor, a few doors down the corridor from mine.

I'd treated myself to a new evening gown for the occasion as the ones I had in my wardrobe were completely out of fashion and destined for the charity shop. I'd chosen a slinky, full length, pale turquoise number with a low cut sequined bodice and thin straps. A lace bolero in the same colour would cover my shoulders and upper arms until I felt brave enough to reveal them.

I'd always enjoyed putting makeup on when I was going somewhere special but it had been a while since I'd had the occasion to do so. I realised I hadn't lost the knack and was pleased with my efforts. Carrie had made me a set of crystal earrings and necklace for my christmas present and they were the perfect accessories. To complete my outfit I'd opted for a low kitten heeled black court shoe with a matching handbag; my days of dancing the night away on three or four inch stilettos were way behind me. Before I rang Dave to tell him I was ready I studied my reflection in the full length mirror on the wardrobe door and was satisfied with what I saw.

I opened the door when Dave knocked and my heart did somersaults when I saw him; he looked so handsome in his tuxedo. For once I was lost for words so he spoke first. "Wow,you look really lovely, Harriet."

"Thank you, you scrub up well yourself," I said.

"I'm glad you think so," he said, offering me his arm.

We were seated at a round table with three other couples; there were streamers and party poppers on the table ready for midnight and four bottles of sparkling wine to see the new year in with a toast. The four course dinner was superb; being such a large gathering we'd had to choose what we wanted from the menu in advance. Dave and I had both opted for steak in diane sauce for our main course and they were cooked to perfection. After the meal I was so full that I didn't think I'd be able to dance but Dave persuaded me and when he waltzed me around the dance floor I felt like a teenager again. "I didn't know you were such a good dancer, I whispered in his ear.

"There are lots of things I'm good at, Harriet," he whispered back, making a shiver run down my back, which you've yet to find out."

My heart missed a beat and something told me that if I played my cards right, the first night of the new year would be one of discovery.

The End

Printed in Great Britain
by Amazon

42549985R00096